NOW OR NEVER

RUTH HAY

To my husband, who has always had the benefit of good timing.

Tempus fugit. Time flies.
~ Virgil

About This Book

Now or Never is the third book in the series, **Prime Time**, which began with Anna Mason's story in Auld Acquaintance.

In this book, two of Anna's dear friends travel to Italy for very different and urgent family reasons.

Will Maria find common ground at the villa with her rebellious teenage daughter before it is too late?

Will Susan persuade her husband, Jake, that a new, unproven treatment for multiple sclerosis may be a risk they cannot afford to take?

Anna helps both her friends from a distance then draws them together for an unexpected event that provides an exciting conclusion.

Chapter One

I t is never good to make decisions based on desperation, thought Maria.

Desperation indicates fear, and fear can be smelled and tasted by your opponent and gives her, or him, an edge in any negotiations.

Of course, in business dealings Maria knew she was the one who would benefit from the desperation of others in the trade. As an experienced store owner, she was adept at the hard sell. She knew when a fashion line was overpriced or just on the point of going out of style.

She would pounce like a cat on a mouse, and emerge from the fray with a van-load of bargains.

Why can't I use that skill with Lucy, she wondered. Is it not possible to be objective and rational when dealing with my own flesh and blood?

Paul insisted that the problems between mother and daughter arose from the fact they were too much alike. Maria always bristled at this accusation. She couldn't see it herself.

Lucy had always been a difficult child from minute one as far as her mother was concerned.

Theresa had been the easy first child. She smiled and cooed as a baby and excused any errors her young parents had made with a benign wave of her chubby little hands. Maria managed to fit Theresa's first years into her own ambitions to apprentice in a small store in the mall. It was this ease that had persuaded her to try for another child and, to Paul's delight, a second daughter was born.

Maria shifted uncomfortably in the driver's seat. The 401 West from Toronto was quiet at this early hour and she sped along smoothly with time to think. If I'm honest, she admitted to herself, it could have been the timing that set us off on the wrong foot. Perhaps five years was too long between children or it was just when I was carving a career that required too many hours at my business. Maybe it was the contrast between the two babies that threw me off.

Lucia was not the child of light that her name promised. Maria sighed as she remembered the long nights rocking a restless baby on her lap. Although Paul was a great father and less busy nowadays with his photography, in those days, it always fell to a mother to hear the cries and wake with a start when the tears began.

It was not until she stopped breast-feeding that Paul could take over at night and Maria began to sleep for a few hours. Paul had a soothing effect on Lucy and the two bonded in the dark hours in a way Maria had envied. A pattern had been established that persisted right into the present. No matter what Maria tried to do, Lucy went first to her father and wheedled him into any crazy scheme she wanted to attempt, from decorating her room in black and white to arranging parties at the house with a group of strange teenage friends. Her mother was always cast in the role of over-cautious objector but, as she was often unavailable to supervise these schemes, Paul's approval and involvement was the simplest solution. Lucy could cause explosive arguments when she wanted her way and over the years it was easier to give in than to fight her.

"I know that was wrong!" declared Maria to the passing cars in the fast lane. "Everything I ever read on child-rearing said the opposite, but what's a working mother to do when she has to earn the money for her family? There are only so many hours in a day and a peaceful household becomes a necessity at the end of a long shift at the store."

She punched the wheel in frustration. It was too late to turn back the clock. The past was what it was. But what about the future?

A service centre appeared on the near side of the road and Maria diverted into the lane that led straight into the parking area. The sun was well up now and she took a deep breath of the cooler morning air as she straightened her back and rested her eyes on the trees surrounding the concrete.

The fall weather had been remarkably mild, and leaves, which should be showing signs of colour by mid October, were still verdant in the warm breeze. Yet, winter was waiting patiently in the wings for its turn on centre stage.

Perhaps there's still time, she thought, as she headed into the restaurant for a latte. I am afraid I will have to do something soon to get closer to Lucy before it's too late.

☙❧

"Look, Lucy! What are you doing here? Go home to daddy and tell *him* your troubles. I have enough to handle, or are you oblivious to that, too?"

Theresa's anger at her sister's selfish behaviour spilled over, despite her usual control. She turned away from the teenager and lifted her young son, smiling to show him the burst of frustration was not his fault. With practiced ease she slid him into the high chair and placed a plastic bowl of dry Cheerios in front of him while she dealt with Lucy's demands.

"Cool off, sister dear!" came the sarcastic reply. "I only came to see if you would support me with mom, for once. You know it's a great idea and it would really help me to get a showcase for my designs. Lots of kids in Arts school are really down with my stuff, you know. I could start selling right away if mom would cooperate."

"What do you expect me to do? Waltz right into her store and tell her how to run her business? You are the one who gets her own way every time, Lucy. Do your own dirty work!"

Theresa stomped out of the kitchen with one quick look back to see Johnny happily making patterns on the tray with his cereal. She had no patience with Lucy. Didn't the kid realize mornings were her busiest time with a baby to attend to upstairs, an eighteen-month old to feed and amuse and a husband's early-morning mess to clean up and all this before the babysitter arrived and Theresa could turn her attention to reaching her part-time office job in something resembling a sane state of mind.

As she changed Francesca's diaper and made happy gurgling noises with her, Theresa's mind was humming on another channel. The nerve of that girl! Coming to me for support with her crazy schemes! As if I care what she does with the weird clothes she puts together from second-hand discards and bits of junk she finds in bins at Goodwill. If she thinks mom will have anything to do with a display of that rubbish in her store windows she's even more removed from reality than I thought she was.

As Theresa picked up discarded socks and swiftly tidied the bed, the baby on her hip worked the usual soothing magic and her mother's anger gradually dissipated. She sat on the edge of the bed while she dressed Fran for the day in the bright colours the baby loved and she talked to her in a sweet tone that was really the self-talk Theresa needed to give herself.

"Lucy just gets my goat, Frannie. I shouldn't let her get to me but this is an old problem with the two of us. If I'm honest, baby, there's a bit of jealousy there. I was the baby of my family once upon a time. Yes I was, sweetheart! I was the apple of my daddy's eye until the screamer appeared on the

4

scene. You won't be jealous of your big brother will you, my darling?

Your daddy and mommy love both of you just the same and my work will never get in the way of your happiness, I promise."

Three deep breaths later and a dozen kisses on Fran's shiny, dark hair and Theresa felt calm enough to descend the stairs to the kitchen. Lucy was picking Johnny's Cheerios off the floor, to his obvious delight.

Theresa almost said, "Don't encourage him, Lucy. He'll do that for hours if you let him and I'll never get him fed!" Just in time, she stopped the words from emerging and decided to play the adult role of the older, and hopefully wiser, sibling.

"You'll need to get off to school now, Lucy. I'll think about what you said but I can't promise anything. Mom's due back from the fashion show in Toronto today. I wouldn't tackle her until tomorrow. She'll have to catch up with things first."

"Good advice, T'resa!" The old childhood name made Theresa smile and she almost gave her sister a hug, but that impulse died when Lucy added, "I thought you could give me a ride to school since mom's away. I'll just finish this coffee and then we can go. OK?"

❦

Maria crumpled the empty cardboard coffee cup but stayed seated in the cafeteria. A few moments of peaceful, quiet contemplation in her busy life were not to be squandered by rushing back to the car for the last few kilometres towards home.

She reviewed the weekend's activities in Toronto. The fashion show at Holt Renfrew was followed by meetings with buyers to discuss trends for the 2011 spring and summer seasons. The more input Maria had gathered, the more confusing the situation became. It looked like another year where the only option would be to declare a 'do your own thing' style. Maria knew this was a cop-out and indicated that no clear direction had emerged from the Paris and Milan shows of the previous spring. Without something new to offer her customers, Maria would have difficulty making a profit. Although she had fashion for a wide range of ages in the store, it was the rich matrons of London who braved the mall's teen crowds to search out Maria's fashion-forward couture. Her wealthy clients saved themselves long trips to New York and Toronto and relied on Maria's personal service and her knack for spotting styles to suit them.

These ladies frequently reported that their out-of-town friends often commented on their outfits during social occasions and winter cruises. When inquiries were made about where they shopped for such elegant clothes, Maria's store was never mentioned and although this did not help her gain more customers, it did mean the ones she had were faithful purchasers who supplied the cash to maintain her stock and her reputation.

Maria closed her eyes and rubbed her throbbing forehead with long, tapered fingers. The headaches were becoming more problematic. Did she need a stronger prescription for her glasses or just to wear them more often? Or perhaps it was the growing list of decisions she had to make that was causing her head to ache like this.

She lifted her BlackBerry from its pocket on the front of her stylish black patent purse and quickly checked the family's schedules. Joe would be home for supper tonight as he was in the studio today. Theresa was at work until 2:30pm and Lucy should be safely at school until at least 3:30pm with some sewing to do for a runway project in February, or so she said.

A jolt of fear struck Maria with this thought. How much could she trust Lucy's word? Young girls today were neither truthful nor dependable. Half the time, their parents never knew what they were up to or who they were with. Maria realized Lucy was wilful, impulsive and determined to fit in with her crowd. She was just the type to fall for some dangerous scheme and be led astray, and lately she was scorning any advice her mother might dare to offer.

There was only one place Maria could head to where problems were unlikely to present themselves and where instant comfort could be found. She could feel the relief rush through her body and diminish the throbbing headache as she returned to the car and merged with the traffic heading to London. It wasn't far to Theresa's little house on the fringes of the city.

The babysitter would welcome a few minutes to tidy things while Maria enjoyed the company of her grandkids. They were so precious. Everything people said about grand-children was true in her estimation. All the fun parts and none of the work and worry, seemed like a good bargain.

Was it guilt that made her love them so? Was she making up for lost time with her own daughters when she stole a few minutes with Theresa's lovely family? Was it just a way to escape from worries at home?

Theresa had been such a different child from Lucy. Even when Maria was working long hours at home, Theresa would seek out substitute mothers in the neighbourhood. Any of the women who were home with a brood of children welcomed the cute little girl who would happily amuse their babies and play nursery games with their toddlers. A quick call to Maria let her know where Theresa had landed and everyone was pleased with the arrangements.

What Joe called, 'benign neglect' had given Theresa a fore-taste of what she was meant to be, a superlative wife and mother to two darling little ones.

Theresa had never displayed any interest in the fashion business. She cherished her family of soft dolls she called her 'babies', and refused to go to sleep at night until all of them were arranged in order of size against the footboard of her bed.

It was easy to see why Theresa had chosen to marry

young. School was not a good fit for her. It was as if she couldn't concentrate on anything that didn't contribute to learning how to be a good mother.

Lucy, on the other hand, had owned only one Barbie doll whose hair eventually fell out from all the braiding and twisting into outrageous styles her owner had subjected it to. As a child she never played with her sister or made friends with the neighbours' children. She was fascinated with the computer and had online buddies from an early age. Only her father's insistence persuaded her to forego extensive tattooing by showing her how embarrassing her future wedding photographs would be if she indulged in the long dragon and snakes patterns she wanted.

And now............... things were not any easier. Education at a School for the Arts had awakened Lucy's creative side and the result was not what Maria would have wished.

She had to admit, however reluctantly, that the girl had her own crazy kind of ingenuity. She seemed to be capable of inventing new and cheap ways of putting outfits together. Maria was constantly surprised by Lucy's attire when she emerged from her bedroom in the morning, heading for school. She had a knack for combining the most unlikely pieces into a different style each day. Maria knew the size of her daughter's closet and often wondered how it held so many tops, pants, skirts and accessories.

Her professional analysis, over years of observation, revealed that Lucy was re-making existing elements to create different looks. A pair of expensive dark-wash jeans purchased by her mother, would evolve into a hand-painted designer pair with the dragons and snakes motifs denied her by her parents. Next they would receive a sparkle accent, and later be cut down to capri length with a bleach wash to lighten the colour and a drawstring hem.

By summer, these would transform into short shorts decorated with coloured patch pockets or draped in long fringes from a variety of unusual belts Lucy devised from old suede ties.

The girl had style all right. Style that was the antithesis of everything her mother loved about fashion. Was this another way of rejecting her mother's influence?

Maria shook her head to release these uncomfortable thoughts. She could see Theresa's driveway ahead. The very sight of that trim front yard brought down her blood pressure and she consciously relaxed her face to prepare for the happy expression her beloved grandchildren expected and deserved.

Chapter Two

Susan's heart sank when she saw Jake's wheelchair rolled up to the desk and the computer screen blinking on another health-related web site. He had always followed events on the multiple sclerosis society's web site, but since this summer's advent of media attention to the new Liberation Therapy treatment developed by a vascular surgeon in Italy with the unlikely name of Dr. Zamboni, Jake had been obsessed with internet news and reports on the subject.

Susan had tried, as delicately as she could, to divert him from what she considered another ploy to engender false hope in the large number of Canadians who suffered from MS. Her own background as a legal secretary for many years had conditioned her to be skeptical about any unproven claims, but she could only present negative information on a limited number of occasions before her husband exploded with frustration at her perceived lack of support and the topic was banned for the duration.

Susan had to admit that the entire situation had caused stress between the two partners. Stress was never good for Jake. His MS was of the more common type that had periods of partial remission but these could be ruined by devastating attacks which were often produced when he was undergoing stress of one kind or another. Susan's own stress level would rise whenever Jake spoke passionately about the latest Canadian to travel abroad and return from the angioplasty procedure with glowing reports of restored health and strength. She was increasingly afraid that her husband would want to invest their limited energy and financial resources in such an expedition. One she simply could not support.

"Oh, there you are Susan!" Jake scarcely diverted his eyes from the screen to acknowledge his wife's arrival but the two big Labradors lifted their heads and wagged their tails as soon as they heard her name. She moved across the kitchen floor and rested her hands lightly on her husband's shoulders swallowing deeply to prepare herself for the inevitable announcements.

"Have you seen this report on a local woman from Stratford who had the procedure in India last August?" Without waiting for a reply, Jake rushed on. "She says here her legs are feeling a lot lighter and she has the sense of warmth in them for the first time in ages.

This is a quote; 'The sky is the limit now for healing. My body is showing me every day something new and it has only been a week'. Only a week! Susan wouldn't that be incredible?

Imagine what a difference it would make to us if I could have the balance to walk easily again.

I could fold this wheelchair and lock it away in a closet for good!"

Susan made conciliatory noises toward her husband's head but all the while she was longing to say that it was too soon to be claiming long-term improvements. Harking back to an old theme she ventured timidly, "Jake, darling, I read that the MS society in Canada has invested over $46 million in cutting-edge research. Wouldn't it be safer to wait until they have their new drug treatments approved and available here?"

Jake swung his chair around to face his wife. The dogs clattered to a safe distance away from the wheels and sat down again to witness the drama their senses picked up.

"Susan, you know how I feel about this. Time is not on my side. After every attack I have, the possibility of recovery is diminished. I am not getting better and you know very well, how much worse I could get."

Jake pulled his wife toward him and gently stroked her arms. "I have to tell you that I am becoming determined to try this new therapy. No, don't shake your head, Susan. I understand your objections and I can't deny the truth of them, but I feel so strongly that this may be my last chance. I want to go to Italy."

༺༻

"Anna! Thank God you are back from Scotland! I really need to talk to you."

"Susan what's up? You don't even sound like yourself. Is Jake all right?"

"Well, he's fine physically but I am beginning to doubt his mental state at the moment."

"What? That can't be! You two are the most stable married couple I know. Get yourself over here right now. It will be nice for me to help you for a change, if I can, of course."

"Are you sure you are not too busy? I need a good friend's listening ear."

"I can promise you two of those ears. Alina is handling the business at the moment and she's at the warehouse this afternoon. I am free as a bird, Susan."

"Would it be all right if I brought the dogs? I don't want Jake to think I am taking our troubles out of the house."

"Definitely! I'd love to see them. I'll expect you soon."

"Thank you Anna. I was hoping I could count on you. Bye for now."

Anna put down her phone and tried to make sense of the

conversation she had just heard. Susan was the go-to gal for the entire Samba group of friends. Susan and Jake were acknowledged to be the happiest married couple around. Their devotion to each other was evident and a contributing factor in Jake's ability to handle his illness so capably.

What could be so wrong with them that Susan was afraid to let her husband know she was asking for help?

Anna sighed at the prospect of an afternoon of problem solving. It was not a role she was familiar with on this side of the Atlantic, although she had developed the skill in Scotland when she was faced with challenges she had never expected in her lifetime.

Susan was the one who had steered Anna through the whole uncertain business of taking a chance on living in a primitive estate house outside Oban. More importantly, Susan had helped to find the identity of the relative who had left Anna the property in the first place.

Anna had lacked the confidence, then, to make the many decisions that were required. Susan's positive influence had made all the difference. Susan was the one the Samba group had always relied on when any legal issues were involved.

Anna ran her hands through her short, bronze cap of hair. No point in standing here worrying she thought. I'll make sure the back gate is closed so the dogs can safely get some exercise and then I'll put on a pot of coffee and set the table with some of those goodies I brought back from Scotland.

Susan made fast time from her downtown location out to the new development where Anna and Alina had recently bought a house in a gated community. They were lucky to buy on the edge of parkland and achieved not only a fine view of tree-lined avenues but also extra space at the rear of the house which descended to a valley where a tributary of the Thames River meandered along the shady bottom. The condominium was spacious and included the custodial services that allowed Anna and Alina to leave their home for Scotland whenever their international A Plus business required their attention. It was a convenient arrangement, Susan thought, and quite a significant change from the separate lives both were living prior to Anna's inheritance.

She reminded herself that Anna was a different person now. In appearance and attitude she had learned to make the best of her circumstances. Susan felt a degree of pride in the transformation as she knew she had had a hand in this new version of Anna.

The Anna in question emerged from the front door as Susan called the dogs out of the rear of her low-slung station wagon. Susan knew it was an old model but it had been converted to accommodate both Jake's wheel chair and a compartment to contain the two large dogs.

Oscar and Dominic raced to Anna's side for a minute of hearty ear scratching on their respective black and brown heads. They were always well behaved animals but more so when they scented that Anna had stocked her pocket with the special dog treats they loved.

"I'll take the boys around to the back, Susan, while you go inside and get settled. Isn't it a gorgeous fall day? We've been so lucky with the weather this year."

Susan just nodded in response and headed into the great room where the kitchen and living areas were lit by sunlight from huge glass patio doors. The spectacular view monopolized the attention of anyone who entered. She saw the table set for coffee and conversation and plopped herself down in an upholstered chair with a deep sigh of relief. She held no illusions about Anna's ability to solve her problems with Jake, but it felt so good to remove herself from the situation and let someone else take the strain for a brief time.

"Right then! The dogs will be happy exploring outside for a while. Pour us each some coffee, Susan, and I'll just wash the residue of dog treats off my hands. Oh, and please eat some of those Scottish cookies and candies. If you don't, Alina and I will be forced to consume them all and believe me, I ate my share while I was in the farm house this visit.

Maria will be annoyed with me if I can't wear my beautiful new clothes any longer."

"Nonsense, Anna! You look wonderful. I swear that Scottish air does you good every time you go there. It's hard to believe how different your life is in such a short time; a new home, a new business with workers on both sides of the Atlantic and the self-catering holiday rental of your renovated house outside Oban. Bev and the boys just raved about the beauty of the setting. She's becoming quite a regular visitor, I hear. How is the romance going?"

"Susan, it's incredible! Alan Matthews is the typical outdoors man, tall and rugged. He spends his days with sheep and cattle but in many ways I think he reminds Bev of the young husband she lost to war. You should just see them together! Bev walks the hills with Alan, and Prince, his sheepdog, loves her. There would have been no romance if Prince had not approved."

"Oh, Anna! I can hardly believe it. Bev and Alan's lives were the exact opposite of each other before they met in Scotland. How do James and Eric feel about this? They had their mother all to themselves for many years."

"James is an independent young man now. He still works for us at A Plus and we are funding a business course for him in England. Eric was a bit surprised at the outset, but he really took to Kirsty, Alan's mother, and the two of them spend hours together. Kirsty is teaching him about the animals and the old Celtic folklore she loves, and Eric has introduced this elderly woman to his laptop computer, would you believe? It's a riot to see the two heads bent over the keyboard and Kirsty taking in every word Eric says."

Susan had visibly relaxed by this point in the conversation, and Anna was pleased to see a smile on her friend's face. She calculated that this seemed to be the right time to introduce a new topic.

"I would adore it if you and Jake could come to Scotland

and see the house and its surroundings and meet the people I've grown to love. Is he well enough to make the journey?"

Susan's expression changed immediately to one of concern, but she could not ignore Anna's delicate way of asking what was troubling her friend.

"I hate to burden you with this, Anna. "

"Look, we are old pals, Susan. You know I will do anything I can to help."

Susan looked down at the table, now liberally decorated with cake and cookie crumbs. Her lips were pursed and Anna could see how hard it was for her to open up."

"Let me start first, my dear. You mentioned on the phone that you were worried about Jake's mental state. What made you say that?"

To Anna's considerable shock, Susan dissolved in tears and the whole story flooded out of her, interspersed with sobs and pauses to wipe eyes and nose. Anna switched chairs so she could put her arms around Susan and she tried not to react with dismay as she heard the unexpected details.

Eventually, when Susan had calmed down a little, Anna had to interrupt.

"Look, I just returned to Canada and although I heard a bit about this procedure in Scotland, I am not up to speed on the details. Why would a logical man like Jake want to risk his life on this mad scheme? It reminded me of that apricot-seed treatment that sent flocks of cancer sufferers to Mexico some years ago. As far as I can remember it was just a hoax to get sick people's money."

"It's not the money, although the expenses would be immense. It's the damage it could do to Jake that worries me the most. Some MS patients have died from this neck and spinal cord vein unblocking and even if he did get temporary relief of his symptoms, what would happen when the inevitable realization struck that it wasn't a permanent cure? It could devastate him, Anna."

"And you say he doesn't care about these dire possibilities?"

"No. I have tried everything I can think of to appeal to his common sense. He wants to go to the clinic in Italy as soon as possible."

"But what do his doctors say?"

"They agree with us, Anna. They quote the Canadian clinical studies that may even produce results in a year or less but Jake just won't wait."

"But, didn't I see on television that Saskatchewan has agreed to fund trials because their population has a very high prevalence of the disease? Wouldn't it be safer to trust our health system to come up with some definitive advice on this?"

"I know! I know you are right, Anna! He just won't listen to any of it. I am going to have to accept that I must take my husband to a hospital in a foreign country where they may kill him."

Chapter Three

❦

Octber arrived and the glorious weather continued. Cooler evenings brought brilliant red colour to the burning bushes and golden leaves could be seen on the less-sheltered side of maple trees. It was still pleasant to sit outside in the afternoon sun and Paul was drawn there to watch light and shade dance across the wooded skyline. When all was quiet he could hear the leaves rustling slightly. It was a sure sign the trees were preparing to drop their burden of leaves in preparation for winter.

Paul was aware that winter would arrive earlier for him than for his family this year. He had not yet told Maria of his plans. She seemed even more tense than usual this month and he hesitated to drop the surprise on her until he had figured out a solution to at least one of her current problems. In fact he was quite pleased with his latest ingenious plot. Of course, Maria could reject the whole idea out of hand but he felt he could possibly persuade her if the timing and the setting were just right.

The opportunity arose on Thanksgiving weekend. Theresa had volunteered to host the family meal on Sunday with copious contributions from her mother's favourite Italian restaurant.

This left Maria with a few hours to spare on Sunday morning and her husband insisted that they take a short drive together while Lucy was locked in her bedroom composing her holiday outfit.

"A drive where?" demanded Maria. "Just let me sit here and enjoy the peace, Paul. We'll be leaving for Theresa's soon."

"It isn't far. There's something I want you to see and I promise it won't take long."

No amount of pleading was going to change her husband's mind, so Maria gave in and allowed Paul to drive her away from their house. She noticed he brought along two of his cameras and she closed her eyes to rest until the photographic expedition should begin.

She had hardly begun to relax when the car stopped and she found herself in an unfamiliar area.

"Where are we? I don't recognize this but it must be close to home."

"Come on, I want you to see this hidden gem. It's a trail on the edge of a new subdivision. This used to be a corn field until recently. We passed it often but the new houses are springing up where the corn grew, and this one wild piece has been left. I spotted it recently and wanted to return to catch the first of the fall colours."

"Just as I thought," moaned Maria. "It's a photographic opportunity!"

"Well, not entirely. I have another agenda that concerns you."

Intrigued in spite of her objections, Maria followed her husband down a sloping pathway. She was pleased to find her smart shoes were not to be ruined by unfinished paving, so she caught Paul's hand and in only a few steps she began to see what had attracted him to this area.

On their left, backyards of a few substantial new houses could be seen behind high mesh fencing, but to the right, plants, bushes and trees were growing freely in a riot of fall colour. Yellow butterflies hovered over purple asters and white wood asters. Seed heads were heavy on golden grasses and milk weed pods. Thistles were beginning to shed their puffs of silk and goldenrod competed with ragweed for any spot that wasn't already filled.

Maria found the names of these plants popped into her mind as she saw them. Years of helping the girls with school projects had supplied her with nature knowledge she rarely needed now, and had forgotten she ever knew.

"This is amazing, Paul! It's so secluded. There's no one around. It's like a private little wild kingdom here."

"I know! It may not last long when more houses are built but let's follow the trail along. Another surprise awaits around the corner, my lady."

Maria chuckled. Paul was such a romantic when he wanted to be. A pity they didn't get much time together like this. She sighed because she knew that was her own fault. No else was to blame for her long hours away from home.

By the time they reached the large pond designated by city planners as a catchment area for storm water, Maria was breathing deeply of the fresh air and smiling widely. The pathway now wound around one side of the pond and the houses had been left far behind. Paul's surprise turned out to be a large flock of Canada geese resting on the surface of the pond with mallard ducks bobbing near the edges. A field of tall grass was to the left now and the pond area was bordered on their far right with willows and sumac and drifts of Queen Anne lace.

They stopped to take in the scene. There was no noise of traffic although Maria calculated they had to be fairly close to a major road. The trees must be blocking the sounds of weekend traffic, she thought.

Paul raised his arms to take a photograph and the watchful geese rose clumsily into the air, first in ones and twos and then in a flock streaming over their heads.

Paul followed the movement with his camera and even Maria could see that he was capturing some very good shots.

"Too bad we scared them off," she said.

"They were probably heading for the farmers' fields near here to feed for the day. They'll return later. Let's go to the raised viewpoint at the head of the pond. I have something to tell you."

Leaning on a sturdy metal frame with the length of the pond before them, Maria began to wonder about Paul's unusual behaviour.

"I am really enjoying this break, sweetheart, but what's all the secrecy about?"

"Well, it's partly what you just said. You really need a break from the daily routine and I have an idea I want you to consider."

"Hold on, Paul! The Christmas season starts soon at the store. I have masses of work to do and I need to cover expenses before the winter sales. You know there's less money around these days and I have to work harder to attract it."

Paul did not reply immediately. He looked at his wife and saw the stress move through her whole body. Only a moment before she had been leaning comfortably gazing at the peaceful scene before them and now she was upright, tense and distracted. She pulled at her clothes and touched her earrings in a gesture Paul recognized as a signal of her distress.

"It's not just your work that concerns me, honey." As he ventured into more problematic territory, Paul put his arms around his wife and held tight, hoping his strength and support would give her the courage to stay still and deal with the issues. "I've seen you with Lucy lately.

No don't say anything! I know how you try to connect with our daughter and I see how prickly she is with you. You create sparks together in seconds and things deteriorate quickly after that.

I also know how much this bothers you, in spite of your denials." Maria's head was shaking from side to side in both acknowledgement and despair at what she knew to be a true assessment of the situation.

She wanted to flee from these uncomfortable facts but Paul's grip strengthened, and after a moment or two she ceased to resist. Without another word the potential battle was over and she slumped into his comforting embrace pushing aside the cameras that dangled around his chest.

"I won't cry! I won't cry!" she asserted, but tears were in her voice. "I am so afraid for Lucy. I see the teenage girls roaming the mall in predatory groups looking for ways to vent their energy. It only takes one bad decision to ruin a life and if Lucy has no mother figure she can depend on, she might well be one of those who makes a fatal mistake. You know how impulsive she is."

"Now, calm down! She's a smart kid with ideas and ambition, much like her mother, I may say! I am sure she'll be fine but I am *not* so sure you will survive the years until she realizes her parents are the most permanent support in her life."

"But what can I do, Paul? I wake up in the middle of the night with the worries that girl gives me."

"I know, I know." Silence ensued while Paul patted his wife's back and waited till her breathing calmed down.

"Now look! I brought you here to suggest a solution not to add to your problems. I want you to take a trip home to Italy."

"What?" Maria's shock was evident in her tone of voice and raised eyebrows.

"Before you say another word, just listen for a minute. We haven't been back to Italy for years now and it's time for you and Lucy to go there together; a mother and daughter trip. Away from the conflicts of daily life, you two can start afresh and spend time getting to know and like each other on a whole new basis. I've thought a lot about this," Paul rushed on while his wife was temporarily stunned and speechless,

".…. and I think it could be a combined holiday and work opportunity for both of you. You can visit family and check out the fashion scene in Milan and Lucy can do a design project for school. You wouldn't need to be away for more than two weeks and it could make all the difference to be in a new environment."

Maria disentangled herself from her husband's embrace and looked at him in amazement.

This was the Paul who had captured her affections years ago when they first met. Outsiders always thought she was the dominant partner in their marriage but Maria knew the silent power of this man who cared so much that he was content to stay in the background observing and helping in many ways and able to surprise her totally as he was doing right now.

"But, but ………. Paul, we said *we* would go to Italy together whenever we could get the time.

You would miss out. That's not fair on you."

"Well, there's something else you don't know. I have to leave next week. I have a commission from Canadian Geographic to shoot pictures for an article on changes to the Arctic environment. I'll be gone for three weeks then returning north a month or so later. It's an important job that could mean further assignments in the future so the house will be closed up until you and Lucy get back."

Maria's mind was racing as she tried to grasp all the implications of Paul's announcement. Her thoughts flew, as they always seemed to do, toward her business situation. How could she leave the store for two weeks?

Superimposed over this problem a mental picture of a scene from her grandparents' village in Italy suddenly presented itself. A warm afternoon in a sleepy garden sitting under the shade of a vine-covered pergola with a glass of wine in hand and absolutely no appointments or schedules to interrupt the peace.

Deep in her gut, Maria felt a longing for escape. The trap

Paul had set was closing and she was beginning to understand how prescient her husband was. This could be the answer to so many problems; a last chance to mend fences with her daughter; a change of scene away from all the distractions of Lucy's peer group; a way to reconnect, with fashion as a common interest. Lucy would love Italy. She had not been there since childhood. I could make this work. I must make this work.

Paul stood silently watching emotions race across his wife's beautiful face. He could almost read the turmoil of her thoughts but the end result was not yet clear.

After a few tense moments Maria turned to her husband and called out his name. She threw her arms around him, drawing him into a fervent kiss. As the ducks rose quacking in protest into the air, Paul and Maria laughed aloud.

This would be a Thanksgiving weekend to remember.

Chapter Four

❧❧❧

Anna Mason cradled a large mug of coffee laced with Bailey's chocolate liqueur. She and Alina had agreed to forego the pumpkin pie this year in an attempt to counteract the extravagance of Anna's most recent stay in Scotland. The drink's sweetness soothed the need for dessert after the turkey dinner, and Anna felt encouraged by the small sacrifice. She really needed to control her weight. When she spent that first spring in the Oban farm house she had much more than food to concern her and a more active life had kept off excess weight, but old habits die hard when returning to a familiar environment.

The need to adjust to two different lives was a problem Anna had not foreseen when she decided to split her time between her two homes. The situation was prompted by choice at first. After the farm house was renovated, she could not bear to leave it completely and so the idea of renting it out as a self-catering facility for families was born. Soon it became a necessity to return to Ontario and deal with her sub-let apartment and see her devoted Samba group again. But when Anna had settled her affairs there, she found herself involved in the new business venture which became A Plus.

From a small start online featuring, primarily, Alina's

hand-crafted knitwear items, the business quickly grew into an international venture.

Anna had discovered the remnants of a cottage industry in Scotland and employed expert knitters to make the forgotten intricate patterns and designs that were once common knowledge in Scotland. Amazingly this development coincided with a renewed interest in knitwear in the fashion industry and whenever a new style was thought up by the partners it seemed to fly from the catalogue to parts of the globe Anna and Alina had to employ an atlas to identify.

Anna chuckled to herself as she remembered the sharp learning curve all this had entailed.

They would have been lost without Bev's James. Anna had only just acquired a cell phone when the need for advanced technology reared its head. She was much more adept now although the speed of change in the world of the web was constantly leaving her in its wake.

Perhaps she would get used to the trans-Atlantic lifestyle in time. Many business travellers had adjusted to it. She was reluctant to consider the choice of one home over the other. They were both so different and both much loved, but the settling-in period was disorienting as she coped with jet lag, weather changes and the gaps in her knowledge of local events and people.

I think I need to read more newspapers and watch British TV when I am in Canada, she decided, but that is more difficult in Scotland unless I am connected to the internet.

"My mother would have said these were millionaires' worries!" Anna smiled as she imagined her mother's amazement if she could have known the way her daughter's life had turned out.

"What's got you so thoughtful, Anna? You must have been miles away. The phone's been ringing in the kitchen. It's Maria. You'd better hurry. She never has much time to talk."

Anna responded to Alina's urgency by heading to the kitchen where she saw that the remains of the Thanksgiving feast had been cleared away by her friend while Anna herself had been dreaming by the windows. Typical Alina, she thought; always stepping in to help.

Anna had meant to contact Maria before now, but the situation with Susan had taken up most of her time lately.

"Maria, how are you? Happy Thanksgiving!

My apologies for not calling you before this, Maria. It's the usual scramble to get back into things when I come home."

"Don't apologize, my dear. We are all so glad to have you here again for a while.

Listen, I can't reach Susan and there's a strange message on her answer phone.

Do you have any idea where she is?"

"Well, that's a long story but she did appoint me to fill you in. The bottom line is that she has gone to that clinic in Italy to find out if Jake is a candidate for the experimental treatment for MS."

There was a long pause after Anna made this announcement.

"Are you still there, Maria?"

"Um, yes I'm here, but I am confused. I had no idea Susan and Jake were even thinking along these lines. When did all this happen?"

"Around the beginning of October, just after I got home. Don't be upset, Maria.

I know Susan meant to call you but she was very conflicted about the whole idea and she was reluctant to talk to anyone until things were settled."

"I'm not upset, Anna, but I am surprised. This is just too weird a coincidence.

Earlier today Paul and I had a long talk and we decided that I would take Lucy with me to visit my grandparents in Italy for a couple of weeks."

"Now, wait one minute! I get home to see my friends and everyone promptly takes off for foreign lands! What have I started here?"

Maria joined Anna in laughter at this thought, but it wasn't so far from the truth.

"It does seem like that, I guess, but I'm sure you and Alina will be glad of time to catch up with your Canadian lives. Do you have Susan's Italian information?

I will try to contact her in case they need any help while I'm there."

"Oh, that's good of you, Maria. I am a bit worried about them. This could be the most important decision of their lives and they are by no means together about it."

No problem! "I'll have to go, Anna. Lots of arrangements to make. Thanks for the info. I'll keep in touch. We do miss you, you know.

Bye!"

Anna turned from the phone to find Alina sitting on a stool at the kitchen island with her cup of coffee in her hands and an expression of anticipation in her eyes.

"What was all that about? You looked like it might not be good news."

"No, it's not *bad* news, just unexpected. Maria is going to Italy with Lucy."

"What? You mean Maria is leaving the store. In October? Travelling with Lucy? In term time?"

"Yes, it does sound unlikely now that you say it out loud. There must be something important at stake. What's happening to everyone, Alina? Is there some sense of panic in the air?

Perhaps it's the thought of winter on the horizon. Birds and friends are flying south."

Maria was back in the store early on Monday morning. If this trip to Italy was to become a reality she had preparations to make. Thank goodness she had not had to host Thanksgiving dinner this year. She would, for sure, have burned something, so distracted was she by Paul's proposal. By mutual decision she and Paul had agreed to delay telling the girls until arrangements were finalized but now the plan had to be put in place.

This was not going to be easy, however. There was Lucy to tackle. Maria could already guess how annoyed her daughter would be at this interference in her life.

Then there was Theresa. Things would have to be smoothed over in that department also, she suspected.

As ever, Maria was seriously concerned about her business. Who could be left in charge while she was away? Short buying trips to the states were not a problem but this trip, at this time, was another story altogether.

Taking a deep breath, she decided to take the plunge and do something she had been considering for several months. The store's assistant manager was an experienced sales person who had proved her competence more than once in the last year. Nova was a bright woman who hailed from Nova Scotia and grew up watching the big ships arrive and depart from Halifax and Dartmouth. Her mother, the originator of her unusual name, said the sights and smells of the sea were in her daughter's blood from a very early age. Nova, herself, claimed she was never content until she discovered there were jobs on cruise ships and she could be paid for sailing away on holidays with pleasant people.

After several years doing a variety of jobs on board, the observant Nova realized the importance of women's cruise clothing and became an expert in cruise wear, eventually moving to Toronto and settling in London when she met her husband.

Maria felt Nova was ready for the responsibility. She could helm a feature week of cruise fashions which fit in nicely with the winter sailing trips to the Caribbean and South America much loved by wealthy Canadian 'snowbirds'. Maria would talk to Nova right away and set things in motion. There would have to be ads in the newspaper and flyers sent out to likely customers and posters for the store windows.

Maria inserted a check mark against the first item listed on her BlackBerry and immediately felt more confident about the next in line.

Who to talk to first was an issue. Lucy would fire up at the very suggestion of spending time exclusively with her mother and she would call on Theresa's support within an hour of the announcement. Better to forewarn Theresa and prepare her for the onslaught. It occurred to Maria at this juncture that something more was required for her older daughter. After all, Lucy was getting all the treats, even if she didn't approve of them, and Theresa would be at home with the usual busy life and all her immediate family off having fun.

Would a new winter outfit compensate for this unintended oversight? Maria conjured up a vision of Theresa's brunette hair and olive complexion flattered by a stylish and practical sky blue parka with soft white fur around the face. A pair of slender navy pants and gorgeous leather, knee-high boots would complete the picture.

Maria stopped herself from speculating further. Theresa was a grown woman with her own taste in clothes. She could choose for herself and any hint of a bribe must be avoided at all costs.

"I know!" she exclaimed to the pile of fabric samples on her desktop. "I'll take Theresa flowers later tonight to thank her for dinner yesterday and I'll tell her about the trip when the children are in bed and she has a chance to relax. We could plan something special together when Theresa has a break from work."

Said out loud, this idea sounded more optimistic than Maria actually believed it to be. She was not unaware that her older daughter harboured some degree of resentment against her sister.

"It's always all about Lucy, Mom!" was a frequent refrain when Theresa's frustration boiled over.

Maria had to admit she was right. Maria was guilty of unloading onto Theresa her annoyance with Lucy's more outrageous ideas, especially when Lucy paraded one of her latest creations right into her mother's store while customers were browsing the racks of fashionable clothing.

Theresa's response was, "You know she only does it to annoy you Mom. You shouldn't give her the satisfaction!"

Easy to say, but much more difficult to do, thought Maria, not for first time. Still, I have to start somewhere with this plan or it will never happen. There's a limited amount of time available before the Christmas season.

☙❧

"Pops! You have to do something! She has finally gone over the edge of sanity into the abyss of pure lunacy. I will not leave my friends and my school work to go trailing after my mother, the control freak, to some village where I know no one and can't even talk the language. I will not go. Tell her!"

"Hold on, Lucy! That's a bit strong even for you. You are jumping to conclusions. This is not your mother's idea. It's mine."

"No way! You don't mean that. You can't mean it! You are making excuses for her, as usual."

"All right! That's quite enough Lucy! You need to calm down and listen to me."

Her father's quiet, steady voice forced Lucy to take a step back and collapse onto the bottom step of the staircase. She had been waiting by the front door for her father to arrive home and worked herself into a red-faced fit of anger long before she heard his key in the door.

Paul took his time hanging his coat in the hall closet and stowing his cameras and papers in the box on the top shelf where they would be safe. He knew Lucy needed some space to pull herself together. She would be embarrassed to remember her outburst once she understood the solid reasons for the trip, from her father's point of view.

"Hop into the kitchen and put one of those frozen entrees into the microwave, Lucy. I've been in meetings since noon and you know I can't function on an empty stomach. Have you eaten?"

Lucy shook her head. Her face was losing the high colour of only moments before and she was becoming uncomfortably aware that she might have crossed the line with her father.

She hurried into the kitchen and scrabbled in the freezer for the least-objectionable of the Lean Cuisine offerings. Organizing the meal for her father and herself distracted her from her furious emotions and by the time she had put out cutlery and drinks, she was ready to sit down and hear what her father had to say.

"Lucy, you know I have to go north next week on an important assignment. What you don't know, is how much I worry about your attitude to your mother. I need a clear mind to do my job well, and lately, thoughts and concerns about you have been monopolizing my concentration."

Lucy put down the fork in her hand and lowered her head. Her beloved father was talking to her as one adult to another adult and she could not ignore his words or his worries.

"Your mother has supported this family for years while I worked to build up my reputation as a free-lance photographer. You do not realize how much of this home and everything you take for granted, depends on your mother's hard work and determination.

It's time for you to grow up, Lucy. You *will* go to Italy with your mother and you *will* help her in any way you can while you are there. I expect you to make an attitude adjustment starting right now and to begin with an apology when your mother comes home tonight."

Lucy's mouth fell open in surprise. Her father never spoke to her in this way. She had always been able to twist him around her little finger whenever she wanted to. This was a new father and Lucy did not know how to react to him.

Before she could decide how to respond, her father softened his tone, smiled, and reached out his hand to cover her own which she realized was trembling in some kind of shock.

"Look at it this way, Lucy-Lou, you get to have a holiday in a beautiful place, meet some family, tour about a bit and even miss some school. Now what's so awful about that?"

Lucy grinned at the baby name her father had used. When she looked at the situation from that perspective, there was some truth in what he said. Surely she could endure her mother's company for two weeks without splitting a gut, and she would be working her way back into her father's good graces into the bargain.

Paul watched his younger daughter with some trepidation. He knew he had chosen to approach her with a different tactic in the hopes she would appreciate his trust in her, but nothing was ever for certain with Lucy. He watched as doubt and surprise took their turn on that remarkable face. She did not yet realize how transparent her emotions were. Paul could see beneath the teenage pout and the exaggerated make-up, the fine bones and remarkable colouring of his wife's Italian heritage. Lucy was going to emerge as an elegant, beautiful woman one day soon and perhaps then she would be more sympathetic to her mother.

Paul saw the moment when Lucy's decision was made.

His shoulders relaxed a fraction in anticipation of a positive result.

"It's a deal, Pops! I'll do my best but I can't promise to like it."

"That's good enough for now. Let's eat! I'm starving!"

Chapter Five

Susan had never felt so uncomfortable and out of her depth in her entire life. She was accustomed to being in charge of most situations but this was something new for her and she did not like it in the least.

First of all, she was not a medical expert although she had learned a great deal from watching Jake as he battled his MS symptoms over the years. She had accompanied him to endless doctor appointments and helped him when he went through the depression that inevitably accompanied a downturn in his ability to cope with deteriorating muscle strength.

On reflection, she recognized that the turning point was when Jake had to accept the necessity of a wheelchair. His feet became so cold that his balance was unsure. He was so afraid of the 'drop-foot' syndrome and his fears began to take over his thoughts.

Through all these stages, Susan had managed to cope quite well, she thought, but now everything had changed.

The support group for MS that Jake had found online had become a militant force, determined to find a way around the Canadian health system's reluctance to prove definitively that CCSVI was, or was not, a genuine factor causing multiple sclerosis. After much debate, the group had decided to visit

Ferrara University and see for themselves whether or not Dr. Paolo Zamboni's procedure could help them.

Susan had allied herself with the spouses and partners of the group who were reluctant to take this action. All of them understood the financial costs involved in a two or three week stay in Italy as well as the possible disappointment that could result from a negative experience.

These concerns, however, paled in comparison to the risk that the MS patients would take if they elected to accept the treatment and undergo the procedure.

Susan had extracted a solemn promise from Jake that he would not take the option of flying off to a clinic in Costa Rico, India or Mexico. She was so afraid of disreputable medical tourism and had tried to persuade Jake to enroll in one of the U.S. clinics but he would not wait any longer. The best she could negotiate was this deal in Italy which the MS group insisted was primarily an investigation at the site of the original discoveries, not necessarily a treatment opportunity.

And so, Susan woke up each day in a small hotel, almost exclusively occupied by the Canadians, a few miles from the centre of Ferrara. She could hardly believe she was here. She tried to keep herself calm by staying away from the hospital as much as possible. The accompanying spouses took turns escorting their partners in a hired van which allowed the others some time away from the fraught atmosphere of the clinic. Susan tried short excursions by bus in the surrounding area but found she could not concentrate on the countryside or the historic old towns. Her mind was preoccupied with worry about what might be decided while she was off trying to enjoy herself.

The talk around the dinner tables each night became more and more enthusiastic as the returning Canadian delegation described the people they had met and the positive stories they had to tell of restored energy and clearer thinking. What bothered Susan the most about this hype was that some of the patients were returning for their second or third vein unblocking and some had stents replaced. She knew enough to understand the danger of blood clots in repeat procedures and her heart missed a beat at the thought of Jake's involvement.

At the same time, she had to admit the group was having a very positive effect on her husband's attitude. It had been years since she had seen him so fired up about his prospects for recovery. After the evening meal, the Canadians sat around reviewing the day's activities and Susan watched in amazement as Jake, who was never able to stay up past 8:00 pm at home, discussed medical details well into the night.

There was only so much of this Susan could stand. She would slip out of the lounge and fetch her coat so that she could sit outdoors. The evenings were a little cool although the afternoons were warm and comfortable.

"Quite like our Ontario Octobers," she said to the moonlit sky as she pulled out her cell phone and speed-dialed Anna's number. Within seconds she heard Anna's voice. They had arranged a convenient time for calls before Susan left home.

"How are things, Susan?"

"Oh, Anna, I've never been so homesick in my life. Every day we spend here is like a month."

"But it's not a bad place you are staying at. Am I right?"

"No, that's not it at all, Anna. Thanks to you, I don't have any money worries at the moment. The accommodation is fine, it's just that I am afraid Jake will get approval for the procedure to go ahead one of these days and there will be nothing I can do about it."

"So he's had all the tests now?"

"Yes."

"You don't sound very confident about the results."

"I think they will say he's a good candidate, whether he is or not. I can't judge if this

place is legitimate. It looks like a regular hospital facility and there are caring people working there but I just don't know. Every day makes the risk worse."

"It sounds like every day adds to your stress, Susan. You need to take care of yourself.

What would happen to Jake if you were to take sick?"

"Don't even go there, Anna. I can't think about the future. I am in limbo here.

Everything, and everyone, I know is so far away."

"Well, I have some cheerful news on that score, Susan. Maria and Lucy are coming to Italy."

"Good grief! Why?"

"Well, Paul decided they both needed some time away and he contacted her family,

then made all the arrangements before Maria had time to change her mind."

"I always said that man was a treasure! I feel better just knowing one of my

Samba friends is within reach. Where are they staying?"

"Maria says they will be at the family villa outside Bologna. She told me to tell you to join them if you can, but if not, she has your numbers and will call soon."

"Anna, you have no idea what a relief it is to hear this. You've given me a ray of hope

in the darkness."

"Good! It wouldn't compare to the help you have given me over the years, dear friend.

Now, get some rest and things will be better tomorrow. Alina sends her love.

Goodnight, Susan."

🌸

The journey to Italy had started more smoothly than Maria had expected. Lucy was exhausted from telling and re-telling the story to all her friends about how she was being forcibly removed from hearth and home to venture forth to a foreign land against her will and without a clue where she would be for *two whole weeks!* Eventually, the friends grew tired of her complaints and told her to get a life, whereupon she turned her attention to choosing clothes for the trip and that had occupied every waking minute until they departed for the ride to Toronto.

As soon as the plane took off, Lucy's head fell back and she dropped into the zombie-like state of oblivion that only teenagers can command.

Maria was delighted. No confrontations for the duration of the plane trip and she could relax.

Under the seat in front of her was a briefcase full of papers, maps and ideas for shopping trips and other places Lucy might enjoy. There had been no time to share this information with her daughter. That would come after they were settled in the villa.

Maria wondered how Lucy would adjust to living in the country without the amenities she was used to in Canada. She would not like sharing a room with her mother, for a start. The villa was occupied by a variety of Maria's older relatives. The number varied from season to season but Maria's mother in Toronto had assured her the aunts were delighted to welcome family from Canada and space would be available for them "*subito!*"

It had been years since Maria had visited the villa in the countryside outside Bologna. The last time was with Paul in the summer. The girls were in Toronto with their grand-mother and all Maria could remember of that holiday was sleeping late in Paul's arms, afternoon naps after huge meals outdoors and more wine than she usually consumed in a year. It was wonderful. Why didn't we come back again, she wondered. Why not? Where does all the time go?

This trip would not be so easy, but Maria was determined to forge a new understanding with Lucy no matter what it took. They would arrive at the Bologna Marconi Airport in a few hours and a short drive by taxi would take them to the old town in the hills.

I hope it all goes smoothly, thought Maria as she drifted off to sleep.

❦

Lucy hardly remembered arriving at the villa. It was dark and there were no streetlights. In fact there were no real streets as far as she could see. The taxi chugged up a winding road to the top of a hill with its load of luggage and each time it went around a bend the road seemed to narrow even more. It was difficult to make out the buildings they passed on the way. The shapes were not familiar to Lucy and she couldn't determine whether they were houses or churches, although she thought there were probably way too many of the latter. There didn't appear to be anything resembling a store that she would recognize as such. It looked like shutters covered all the windows and everyone was asleep early.

Finally the taxi stopped. Her mother got out of the car to pay the driver and Lucy walked toward the steps in front of the large door in the wall that stretched to her left and right and rose upward for two more storeys. There was a dim lantern over this door and lights in some upper level windows, but when the door burst open in front of her she was dazzled by a blaze of electric light from the interior and before she could step back she was engulfed in the strong arms of three old women who exclaimed over her, patted her cheeks and kissed her over and over. All she could understand from their excited speech was, *"Bella Lucia! Bella Lucia!"*

After she had been forcibly passed around the group one more time, a younger woman took her hand, separating her from the trio who now turned their attention to Lucy's mother.

Pointing to herself and saying, "I am Angela," the woman

40

led Lucy up a stone staircase to a bedroom and, smiling widely, she left the room stating that she would return soon.

Lucy could hear loud chatter coming from the lower level but as she could not understand one word, she turned from the door to see what the room contained, other than the one large bed with a shiny brass railing at the head of it. She quickly decided there wasn't much more to see.

A low bench, padded with worn cushions, sat under each of the shuttered windows. There was a wooden dressing table with a huge, ancient mirror balanced on top, a carpet under the bed covering only part of the stone floor and on one wall, a narrow door. Through this she found a cupboard for clothes and a small washroom with a bath and no shower.

While she was washing her face and hands she heard the noises of the bedroom door opening and cases being placed on the floor. By the time she had found the towels and dried her hands, the room was empty again.

No mother appeared, so Lucy lay down on the bed to test its softness. Her head sank back into two oversized pillows and before she had realized that she was sharing this bed with her mother, she had fallen into a deep sleep.

❁

Hours later, Lucy's eyes sprang open. At first she panicked. Nothing was familiar in the half-dark of the room. Where was she and what had awakened her? She pushed the cover aside and found she was still dressed in her travel clothes minus the shoes.

A low moan coming from her right alerted her to the fact that she was not alone in the bed.

After a brief moment of horror, she recognized her mother's face under a tousled mass of dark hair. Leaving the bed without waking her mother was top priority, so Lucy slid quietly out at her side of the high bed and feeling around with her bare feet, she found her shoes.

She debated whether she could use the washroom and decided the thick door would muffle any noises. A quick splash with cold water, chased away the last of her confusion and a moment later she was out of the bedroom and heading down the stairs on tiptoe.

"Sure saves time in the morning when you don't have to get dressed first," she murmured to herself, and discovered a sense of anticipation welling up as she contemplated exploring this new place on her own. She searched her memory for clues about the villa but she could hardly remember any details from her previous visit as a child. A vague sense of space and open country was all she could summon. As for the old women in the villa, she thought the identical ancient crones had been there the last time, looking exactly the same, although that hardly seemed possible.

The huge front door was barred but not locked. A survey of the simple mechanism revealed that it could be opened easily and quietly. No one was in the open kitchen nearby so she slowly raised the heavy wooden bar and let it swing down out of the way.

Escape was on her mind but escape where? She was stuck here for an endless amount of time and an hour without her mother's company seemed a good start to the endurance race.

She soon found a way around the building leading to the back of the property. Peering into the French doors she saw the kitchen again but as it was still empty she moved to the patio area where a huge table with an assortment of wooden chairs rested under a canopy of leaves trailing over an old frame. No one would see her here and she could look around without being disturbed.

The morning air was cool and a mist blanketed the valley below the villa. Lucy pulled her cell phone out of her pocket and checked the time. It couldn't be 2:00am she thought; there's some light in the sky. Then she remembered the time difference between North America and Europe.

"No point in phoning home yet," she concluded reluctantly, "but I can text my gal pals, although they won't be able to respond for hours."

It felt strange to be so out of touch. The lifeline to her school friends was a compensation that usually kept her sane when things at home got out of hand. She could always count on a sympathetic text or two to cheer her up and assure her she was not wrong in her outrage at her mother's demands. Privately, Lucy believed none of her friend suffered interference the way she did. Their mothers were not on their case every minute of the day like *her* mother was.

This thought caused acid to roll into Lucy's stomach. How was she going to survive this trial?

If they couldn't get along together at home with her mother out of the house a lot of the time, how on earth were they going to manage in each other's close company for weeks?

Shrugging off this grim thought, she leaned back against the wooden struts of the uncomfortable chair and watched as the first rays of sunshine evaporated the mist.

Now she could see a grove of small trees advancing down the slope. Could they be olives or vines? There were no houses nearby. The town must be on the other side of the hill. She was just wondering if this house was the highest around when a noise from behind her caused her to sit up suddenly, overturning the chair which proceeded to deposit her body onto the paved patio.

Before she could cry out, a strong pair of hands appeared under her armpits and she was lifted up into another chair. Someone tall removed the offending chair and simultaneously apologized in English.

"I am so sorry. That chair should have been used for firewood long ago. It has never been steady. Are you all right?"

Lucy opened her mouth to reply and found she was staring at an attractive young man with a concerned expression on his tanned face.

"Where did you spring from?" she asked.

43

"Allow me to introduce myself," he replied, with a partial bow which shocked Lucy more than his sudden appearance had done. "I am Maurizio. The old aunties asked me to look after you this morning before I go to school in Bologna. I have coffee in my Vespa. Wait one minute!"

Maurizio vanished around the end wall of the villa and Lucy tried to pull herself together in the attempt to improve on the clumsy first impression she had given this stranger. He must be older than me she thought, but he is a definite bonus this morning.

Maurizio returned with two coffees in containers, much like the Starbucks Lucy was familiar with at home.

"Where did you get these?" she inquired.

"Ah, there's a small café in town. I always buy one there in case the road to Bologna is busy and I have to wait in a queue."

As she removed the lid from the fragrant coffee, Lucy realized how hungry and thirsty she was.

She took a quick sip and complimented her companion on his excellent English.

"*Grazie, Lucia!* I am studying English Literature for my Comparative Literature degree. I will converse with you in English, if you don't mind."

I don't mind at all, thought Lucy, as she automatically pushed her shoulder-length hair into its most flattering, face-framing style. It was then she remembered how gross she must look. Her make-up was washed off, her hair was hanging free of the essential glossing product and she was wearing the travel clothes she had actually slept in.

Lucy surreptitiously pulled down her jeggings and lowered the zip on the awful sweatsuit jacket she was wearing so that the cute lace-trimmed top underneath would at least give a hint of the style she usually favoured.

Maurizio hardly seemed to notice, however. He was checking his watch and making his apologies for leaving so soon.

"I must go now, Lucia. I will see you soon, no?"

"Yes, definitely!" replied Lucy. "Thanks for the coffee, Maurice."

Oh, God! I even messed up his name, she shuddered inside, concealing the gaff with her biggest smile. Maybe he didn't hear me? I hope not. She lowered her head while the blush receded from her cheeks and she did not dare to look up until he was gone.

❦

"Oh, there you are Lucy! I was wondering where you got to. You were sound asleep when I got upstairs last night so I didn't want to wake you. How are you feeling? How did you get coffee? The *zii*, that means aunties, are just firing up the espresso maker now and the smell is divine."

Lucy tried to focus on her mother's questions but she was still dazed by the vision of Maurizio with his athletic build under a leather bomber jacket and those beautiful dark eyes complimented by equally dark hair and eyebrows. She was already planning to wow him at their next meeting with a totally transformed version of the gruesome hag he had just met.

"Uh, I'm fine. Maurizio brought the coffee. Who is he?"

"Probably one of the cousins, Lucy. There are so many of them I can't keep track.

Can I get you some breakfast? A lightly-scrambled egg perhaps?"

"No thanks. I think I'll go for a shower now. I need to wash my hair and change my clothes."

With this brief statement, her daughter disappeared through the patio doors.

Maria breathed a sigh of relief. She had been expecting a litany of complaints from Lucy starting with the sleeping arrangements, including the lack of a shower, and ending with the isolated location, but as that had not transpired,

45

Maria had a space to refine the itinerary for the next few days. She pulled out the folders she had brought and concentrated on locations that might amuse or interest her daughter. Everything depended on making this time together as pleasant as possible. Her own business agenda must take second place to winning back Lucy's trust and affection.

Chapter Six

❧❧❧

"**S**usan, it's Elaine. I'm calling from the hospital. You'd better come right away.

Jake has had some kind of collapse. I can't understand the details yet, but he is unconscious. Get a taxi. It will be faster than waiting for me to bring the van back."

Susan's first thought was gratitude that she had not wandered off from the hotel this afternoon, and that she had kept her cell phone on while dozing outside in the sunshine.

She quickly stood up and grabbed her purse from the side of her chair, praying that Signora Margherita, the hotel manageress, whose English was good, would be available to help her get a taxi. Every word of Italian that Susan had acquired in the last three weeks had flown from her mind in the panic she was now feeling.

What if Jake died before she could reach him? What if his last memory of her was the fight they had had that morning? What if she was right and this whole crazy enterprise was doomed?

What if she was stranded here with a body to deal with?

This last dire thought shook Susan to the core. What was

she thinking? She had no idea what the situation with Jake actually was. Why was she jumping to conclusions and imagining worst-case scenarios? She should be concentrating on Jake, not on herself.

Somehow she had reached the hotel office where she found the signora bent over her computer keyboard. In a few seconds the older woman had understood the urgency of Susan's request and contacted a local man who would drive her to the hospital.

It was the longest ride of Susan's life. Every time the driver braked for any reason, her heart beat so rapidly she thought it would burst from her chest. She was experiencing guilt, fear and anxiety in increasing measures.

The ten-minute journey in the mid afternoon through relatively-quiet streets to the centre of town was without incident despite Susan's dread of any delays. She did not breathe deeply, however, until the hospital buildings loomed above them.

As soon as the car stopped, she threw open the door, shouted a fervent *"Thank you!"* and fled through the hospital's heavy double doors to the interior. It was only then she realized the driver had taken her to a different entrance than the one where the Canadians usually arrived at Dr. Zamboni's clinic.

Now began a nightmare race through the hospital's corridors to reach the opposite side of the facility. Every time she thought she was heading in the wrong direction again, she would grab the arm of the nearest person and say, "Please, Doctor Zamboni?" Her state of panic must have been obvious as she always received a pitying look and a pointed hand indicating the correct way to go.

At last she saw the clinic's sign and rushed forward falling into Elaine's arms, too exhausted to speak.

"My God, Susan, you look awful! Sit down here and catch your breath. I just checked with the nurse and Jake has recovered consciousness. He is asking for you but you can't see him in this state. You'll only make things worse for him."

Elaine told Sylvia to get a cup of water from the dispenser, and as soon as Susan had sipped the cool contents she dipped a handkerchief into the remaining water then patted Susan's overheated face until she had calmed down.

"Tell me what happened to Jake. "

As Elaine and Sylvia exchanged glances over her head, Susan tried to assure them that she was much better now and could take the truth, whatever it was.

"Well," began Elaine, hesitantly, "we were all in the waiting room watching television until the nurse supervisor could tell us the results of last week's tests. Someone switched from the Italian version of the Y&R that we were watching and laughing at, like we always do, and there on the screen was a documentary in English about Chronic Cerebrospinal Venous Insufficiency.

We all stopped laughing and moved closer to the television so we could hear every word."

"So, what does that have to do with Jake's collapse?" Susan looked from one face to the other seeking an answer. Sylvia was the one to reply to her request.

"Look, Susan, we had no idea what the program would say about the liberation therapy. If we had, we would have turned the whole thing off before our guys and gals heard it but by the time we understood the message they were giving, it was too late."

"Too late for what? What are you talking about?"

"It turns out that a Canadian man has died from the procedure. That's the bottom line and that's what shocked Jake so much."

"Someone died? Here? Recently?" Susan's reaction was impatience with the slow drip of information she was being fed.

"No, no it was a clinic somewhere in Costa Rica. The patient had a balloon angioplasty like Jake wants, but it didn't work, so he requested a stent to open up the veins. His wife said he died of a blood clot."

"The poor woman! How horrible for her. Can you please take me to see Jake now?"

Elaine and Sylvia were glad to hand Susan over to the care of a nurse who was stationed by Jake's bed in a treatment room.

Jake's eyes were closed but he opened them as soon as he heard his wife's voice.

"I'm fine, Susan. Don't worry. I'll be out of here as soon as you are ready to go."

Susan could not speak for fear her tears would overwhelm her but she gave Jake a head-to-toe inspection and noted the normal colour in his cheeks. She could not see any tremors or twitches so she bent down and delivered as gentle a hug and kiss as she could summon, given her huge sense of relief at his survival.

One long look between them was all it took to ask and receive forgiveness for any stress each had subjected the other to in the last weeks.

"What upset you so much when you saw the TV program, Jake? You are not easily affected by bad news once you have made up your mind about a direction to go in."

"It wasn't the news about the poor guy's death that got to me. The interviewer showed a clip of Dr. Zamboni 's response to the news of the man's death and it was his comments that struck me the most."

"What did he say?"

"Well, he was more cautious than we have heard up to this point, Susan. He said stents were not preferred and patients should wait until further clinical trials are completed."

"But, that's not news to you, Jake. Why were you overcome by this televised information?"

Susan watched as Jake passed his hands over his face and then rubbed them through his hair.

"I guess it all hit me at once. The excitement of being here and seeing people with improvements then finally understanding that I might end up worse rather than better, and, most of all, Susan, the strain we have been under because of our disagreement about the whole venture. It just seemed too much to bear. I think I fainted."

"Well, if that's all it is we can thank our lucky stars! I nearly had a heart attack on the way here thinking you were in real trouble."

Jake reached out and Susan lay down beside him on the narrow bed. The feeling of closeness was one she knew well; one that had been absent since their arrival in Italy.

"I think that's what bothered me the most," Jake continued. "I could see what the daily stress was doing to you and I hated the distance between us. I can't continue to pursue something that affects my wife and principal supporter in such a negative way."

After a long embrace that felt like balm poured over Susan's body and soul, she found the strength to look for the positive again.

"Right, Jake! We're not giving up. We just need to wait for conclusive results and follow the trials in Canada. I want you to get a thorough check up from the doctors here and then we'll decide on the next step. Whatever that is, we'll do it together, I promise you."

⚙

"Susan, is that you? I've been trying to reach you for two days now. Is Jake OK?

Did he get the angioplasty? How are you both?"

"Anna, I'm so sorry for worrying you. I turned off the phones. We really needed some time to recover from everything that's happened here."

"But, what…?"

"Sorry again, Anna. Jake is fine and I am fine. It's just that the

whole experience has been exhausting and we had to get back into synch with each other."

"Ah, that makes sense. I know how unhappy you have been. Are you heading home?"

"No, that's not an option immediately. Jake has had a relapse. It's what I feared would happen once the excitement had died down."

"How is he, Susan?"

"Don't worry, Anna. He just needs some time to rest and recuperate before the trip home."

"Of course, but wouldn't you both feel better away from the clinic environment?"

"I couldn't agree more, Anna. I have very mixed feelings about this place. The truth is, the money is running out. This hotel is cheap enough for now. We can't consider anything else."

"I won't allow that, Susan. You know you can call on me for help with expenses. You can't risk Jake's recovery. The journey home will be stressful enough."

"You have helped already, Anna. I can't ask any more of you."

"You are not asking. I am volunteering. Stay put for another day or so. I have an idea. I'll be in touch soon."

Before Susan could protest further, Anna was gone.

A huge wave of homesickness washed over Susan. Just hearing that familiar voice was a comfort and a hope for the future. No struggling with unfamiliar Italian phrases; no need to explain. Anna knew what was needed. Just as all the Samba friends understood each other on a level deeper than thought. Susan had no idea how, or when, they would get home, but for the first time in days she relaxed. Anna had taken over the 'boss' role that Susan had always assumed for the group and she had to admit, it felt good to be on the receiving end for once.

Lucy was up bright and early the next morning. Her dark - brown hair was freshly washed, which was not easily accomplished without a shower, and she had applied the gel gloss that made the uneven ends of her blunt cut separate from each other and swing attractively around her high cheek bones whenever she moved her head. She practiced this movement in the mirror above the sink to get the best effect.

Her make-up was immaculate. Pale skin and dark red lipstick provided the initial contrast but her eyes were the magnet. Minutes had been devoted to careful blending of highlighter and shadow and multiple coats of black mascara outlined her hazel eyes. The effort was definitely worth the trouble, she thought, as she slipped out to the patio in the half-light to await Maurizio's arrival.

While she waited, she pulled out the neat video camera her father had given her. It flipped open quickly and was no bigger than a cell phone but it could take an hour's worth of good-quality video and she had promised her father to make use of it.

Her plan was to set it up on the table, get a shot of herself and Maurizio and then capture the

scenery as she rode on the back of the Vespa scooter to his university in Bologna.

Her mother had agreed to this expedition after Maurizio had presented the idea the night before. Lucy had expected an argument over the scheme but her mother insisted it fit right in with her own plans as she had to pay a courtesy visit to her elderly grandparents, *Bisnonna* and *Bisnonno*, who lived nearby.

Lucy was delighted to get out of this obligation. The three aunties were quite old enough for her to deal with. She crept around the villa as quietly as a mouse so they would not find her and grab her in their wrinkled old arms at every opportunity.

Lucy's sharp ears caught the sound of the scooter's motor. She could hardly wait to see Maurizio again. When the girls back home saw this video of the two of them they would be purple with envy. Even the thought of a late lunch with her mother in Bologna could not dampen Lucy's enthusiasm. She would have hours to spend with Maurizio this morning.

"Ah, there you are, Lucia! I have coffee for us but if you are ready to go, we'll get on the way now to miss the traffic and have our coffee later."

Lucy agreed with this plan and stood up so Maurizio could get the full impact of her hair, make-up and outfit. She had chosen a tight pair of black leggings clinging to her slender legs, a pair of Ugg boots on her feet and a long black sweater under a pink padded vest. The sweater was one her mother's friend Alina had made, and was about the only thing in their online knitwear catalogue Lucy would ever dream of wearing, but she liked the contrast between the black and pink elements of her clothes. Later she would unzip the vest and reveal the antique silver necklaces that spilled down the front of the sweater in a waterfall of chain accents.

To her disappointment, Maurizio did not seem to be impressed with Lucy's preparations. He led the way out to his scooter and handed Lucy a huge black dome of a helmet.

Now this was not something I calculated on, she thought with a grimace. My hair will be ruined by this monster. I wonder if he will let me ride without it?

Maurizio correctly interpreted Lucy's expression and explained, "I am so sorry, Lucia. Your mother insisted that you must wear the helmet or you could not be my passenger."

I might have known she had something to do with spoiling my fun, Lucy groaned silently.

She slid the helmet onto her head as carefully as she could but found a mouthpiece covered the lower part of her face and a visor popped down to shield her eyes.

Lovely, she thought. I might as well be in a suit of armour. Thanks mother!

Lucy's dream of clinging closely to her handsome Italian

while they zipped down the highway, the envy of all they passed on the way, was rapidly dissolving into a nightmare. She had imagined a motorcycle, but discovered the scooter was more like a child's toy. She had to sit upright and although she could hold on to Maurizio's leather jacket, the helmet prevented her from getting too close. The video shooting was also an impossibility under these conditions.

Not starting out well, at all, she concluded.

As soon as they began to wend their way down through the old town, Lucy realized that, despite its appearance, the scooter was a speed machine and it took all her concentration to stay in place on the banana-type seat while they leaned from side to side.

As they approached the motorway, she began to appreciate the blocking effect of the despised helmet as it obscured the proximity to other traffic speeding by on the road. Rules of the road seemed to be quite frighteningly different from the marked lanes and polite driving in Canada. Every time a horn sounded in her ears, Lucy jumped, and then had to readjust her position so as not to be deposited on the paving that was flying by under her feet.

There was no chance of conversation. Lucy was reluctant to distract Maurizio from the job of steering deftly between and around cars, trucks and other scooters. She noticed other girl passengers with hair flying, coffee in hand, and caught scraps of their laughing conversation as they zoomed past. One attractive pair of girls in short skirts even exchanged a comment with Maurizio. Probably laughing at the sight I make here, she thought. When will this end?

Eventually, buildings loomed in the distance and the fields and farms of the countryside became parks and gardens. They passed through a towering arch decorated with sculptures which actually caused the traffic to slow down temporarily and allowed Lucy to catch her breath. She could feel sweat gathering on her hairline and longed to be rid of the helmet.

The university buildings were nearby. It was a complex of ancient, mismatched, ivy-covered ruins to Lucy. They looked nothing like the elegant, pale stone structures of the university in London that she had seen from Western Road. She had little time to compare, however, as Maurizio quickly found a tiny parking spot in a small area beside one of the buildings.

Lucy gladly untangled herself from the scooter seat and tried to disguise the fact that tension had cramped every muscle in her legs and arms. She pulled off the offending helmet and watched as Maurizio casually looped it over the handlebars. A quick glance confirmed that there were no other helmets in evidence.

Well, I guess I could always spot which scooter I came on even in this mass of similar scooters, she thought with a sigh. For the first time she was happy to be returning to the villa with her mother and not with Maurizio.

"I'd better make the best of the time we have together," she exclaimed, not realizing she had spoken aloud.

"Mi scusi, Lucia? Are you well?"

"Oh, it's nothing Maurizio. But I really need that coffee now."

Chapter Seven

✦✦✦

Maria sat at a table in the Piazza Maggiore with a coffee and a glass of water in front of her.

Lucy would be joining her in an hour or so but for now she had time to sit and watch the passing crowd as they marvelled at the magnificent basilica, and the grand palazzos and walked the covered porticos admiring the luxury goods on display.

Paul had been so right, she mused. This time away was a brilliant idea and I really am hopeful that Lucy and I can connect at last. She has been reasonably polite to me recently and I am sure that she will like my travel plans for us in the next few days.

She shuffled the folders again, considering, between sips of coffee, which tour would appeal the most. Florence would be the most educational, of course, but Lucy might prefer Venice.

Rome was too far to go from here and really deserved a separate holiday to do the ancient city justice. The mosaics at Ravenna were not too far away but would Lucy want to tour old churches?

Maria looked up at the formidable basilica with its huge doors built on a scale to intimidate any sinner who might enter. She couldn't see her daughter appreciating this type of architecture.

It was likely to mean an argument if Maria insisted on touring the usual tourist sites.

A new tactic could have the potential for more success with Lucy, she thought. What would work for a teenager? Fashion is something we both have in common, although we each have a completely different vision of what fashion is about.

"Here I am in the midst of the best shoe shopping city in the whole of Italy!" she declared, to the surprise of an elegant couple who were passing her table. Maria noticed that they nodded their heads in approval at her statement. A good sign that I am on the right track, she decided.

Even if their clothing styles did not correspond, Lucy could hardly complain about looking around the footwear shops on every street in Bologna. There were outlet stores and both shoe chains and independent manufacturers nearby, drawing their stock from the many factories in the villages around Bologna.

Maria remembered that Lucy had admired a treasured pair of purple suede boots bought on her mother's last trip to Italy. This could work, she realized, with a feeling of confidence that had been lacking until now. I know my way around fashion and I do have to do some business for the store while I am here. Lucy may not respect me as a mother but she does value my skills as a business woman even if she doesn't acknowledge them very often.

Maria started a new list on the back of one of her folders.

- Lunch, then shoe shopping in Bologna followed by window shopping in the Ugo Bassi arcades before the cab ride home.
- Day trip to Milan for serious high-fashion, designer clothes.

Lucy would love the stores around the Piazza del Duomo and Italy's leading department store, La Rinacente, was located there.

Maybe Lucy would like to walk to the Corsa di Porta Ticinese where there were funky boutiques and vintage shops?

Maria's list grew longer as she became more excited at the prospect of finally sharing her love of fashion with her daughter.

"Why didn't I think of this before?" she chided herself. "If we can't connect here in one of the world's fashion capitals, we can't connect anywhere. This would never work for Theresa, but it must work for Lucy. It must!"

"What's that you're saying about me? What must work? I thought we were here for a holiday."

Maria looked up and found her daughter standing beside her table.

"How did you get here so soon?" she asked. "I wasn't expecting you for another hour or so."

"Huh!" Lucy plopped down onto a chair and grabbed her mother's water glass.

"Things didn't work out the way I wanted with Maurizio," she complained between gulps of water. "He dropped me off a minute ago and was I ever glad to be shot of that awful Vespa! It's a horror story and that helmet you made me wear did nothing for my hairdo, believe me."

Lucy's complaints were part of her usual tactic of distracting herself from the real problems that worried her. On this occasion she was trying to get to grips with the shock of discovering that her stylish outfit for the trip to Maurizio's university had fallen flatter than a pancake when she saw the style of the female Italian students. No one wore pink, or any bright colour, and even when she removed the offending vest and stuffed it under her arm, her black outfit was nowhere near the sleek, tailored slacks and leather boots worn by the majority of students. Strangely enough, her long knit sweater seemed the right style to fit in with the crowd, but she had to swiftly unclip the cascade of silver necklaces and stow them in a pocket since not one student wore any jewellery other than discreet gold earrings, or silver hoops, and large man-styled watches. No tattoos or nose rings were in evidence. Lucy was grateful, for once, that her parents had placed these adornments on the forbidden list while she was still in junior school.

Lucy had never felt so out of place in her life and she had made excuses so Maurizio would cut short the planned tour of the university and take her into town.

☙❧

Well at least she can't run away, thought Maria as she contemplated her daughter's disgruntled expression. I have a captive audience and I will make my pitch as soon as she has had some food.

Throwing caution to the wind, Maria called over a waiter and ordered panini and gelato for them both. The restaurant was notoriously expensive and not a place she would have chosen to eat but the opportunity to change Lucy's mood had presented itself and Maria knew better than to miss this chance.

Over lunch, Lucy warmed to her mother's suggestions and seemed willing to explore fashion Italian style. Her real bout of enthusiasm startled Maria and came from a most unexpected place.

Lucy was glancing over one of Maria's maps as she finished her raspberry gelato when she almost choked on the ice cream and grabbed at her mother's sleeve.

"How do you say this name?" she insisted.

Maria turned the map around almost tearing it to get it out of her daughter's grasp.

"That's San Gimignano. It's a medieval town not too far from the villa. Why? What's got you so excited?"

"Mom, it's the place! It's where they filmed the crucial

60

scenes at the end of the movie. Can we go there? Please can we go there?"

"Sure, we can go there but I didn't think you would be interested in sightseeing, Lucy."

"But this is the same town shown in New Moon. You must see how important *that* is!

My friends at school would faint to be there where Edward nearly died and Bella saved him at the very last minute. We watched the DVD at home that night. Don't you remember?"

Maria had a vague memory of sitting down late one evening to watch something with Lucy but she had fallen asleep long before the ending. She did, however, recall that it was the Twilight series of books that had been made into movies and caused all the girls to go crazy for a vampire named Edward Cullen.

"Oh, right!" she said with a nod of her head but she needn't have worried, Lucy was not about to require more details of her mother. It was sufficient to know that they would be going to the actual site soon.

Maria suddenly realized this was the new development she could capitalize on since Lucy was so enthused about movies. She scanned the map again with a new focus. What movie places might be of interest to Lucy? She discarded several locations immediately. Lucy was too young to have seen some of the classic movies that she and Paul had enjoyed together. What had appeared in cinemas recently?

What about Verona? If Lucy did not appreciate the setting for Shakespeare's tragedy Romeo and Juliet, perhaps she would be more interested in the movie "Letters from Juliet".

"Would you like to see Verona?" she asked tentatively.

"Do you mean it? The real Verona where girls actually post letters and a team of women send advice and answers all over the world?"

For once, Maria had her daughter's full attention. For once they were having a civil conversation and Maria could provide something her daughter needed and wanted. Maria almost cried with the sheer emotional relief of this novel experience.

"Oh, I think we can manage it!" she managed to force out from her constricted throat.

"I haven't seen the movie myself so you will have to fill me in. I take it these are love letters from young girls?"

Lucy became even more animated as she described the movie to her mother. She had watched the special footage on the DVD a number of times with her school pals and they knew, and could quote, whole sections of the dialogue.

"Oh, this is going to be so cool!" she concluded. "I can use Dad's Flip video. Did you know the number of letters to Juliet has doubled since the movie came out? I read about it online."

All thoughts of Maurizio disappeared in a haze of excitement as Lucy imagined the impact of her video on the gals at school and the new, exclusive, European look she would be wearing on the video after the shopping expeditions her mother had planned.

Maria began the shoe trek right after lunch. She didn't want to waste a moment of this new and improved attitude of Lucy's. They even linked arms as they walked along the streets and Maria kept up, despite her growing fatigue, when Lucy found more and more shops to visit.

The bags with their purchases grew heavier as the afternoon sunshine dimmed towards sunset.

Lucy had fallen for a gorgeous pair of black leather boots, a dazzling sequined sneaker and the requisite suede high heels. The latter took considerable time to select as the colours were so brilliant.

In the end, Maria said "Take two pairs, Lucy! I can't choose between them either!"

Super-laid-back-Lucy jumped up and hugged her mother at this generous gesture and once again, Maria had a hard time restraining her tears. She could not remember the last occasion when her daughter had been so spontaneous, or so genuinely happy in her mother's company.

Laden with parcels, they could not go too much farther, but a cab to Ugo Bassi dropped them off at a family restaurant where they ordered pizza after a long discussion about which type of crust and which fillings were preferable.

"How come you can read Italian but you don't speak it much?" asked Lucy after Maria had given their order to the young waiter.

"I can understand what's said," replied Maria, "and I can read anything if I say it aloud in my head first, but I don't get the chance to speak the language much now."

"Didn't you learn Italian from your mama and papa when you were growing up in Toronto?"

Maria realized she had never talked to her girls about the time in Toronto after her parents had immigrated. She had taken it for granted that her parents had told them about those first years during visits to their Little Italy home when the girls were younger. Maria figured it was time to fill Lucy in on some family history.

"You need to understand that immigrant families have many decisions to make when they arrive to settle in a new country," she began. "Your grandparents wanted their children to be a part of Canadian society as soon as we went to school. Some of our friends attended Italian school on Saturdays to keep up the old language but our parents preferred to let us take part in sports and hobbies on the weekends and there was always homework to do."

Lucy's eyebrows raised at this. Homework, other than art projects were never a favourite part of her weekends.

"My mama and papa talked to each other in Italian at home, of course, especially when they had a disagreement they didn't want us to know about, or when one of them was so annoyed with us they burst into a flood of rapid Italian that none of us could follow. We learned the language by osmosis because we were immersed in it but we were never encouraged to converse with each other in Italian. Mama would say, 'English please! English!' "

Lucy thought this over as she dipped bread sticks in plates of spiced olive oil and looked around the restaurant at the long tables where whole families were eating together and talking rapidly with many strange hand gestures and much laughter.

"It seems to me that people should keep their culture alive when they move to another place. We're always hearing about the multicultural society in school. Some of my friends could speak two or three languages before they came to school and the internet says the jobs of the future will depend on the ability to do business across continents and language barriers."

Maria had never heard her daughter speak so eloquently before. This had been a day of surprises for both of them, she thought.

Two large pizzas arrived at their table and brought her train of thought to an abrupt halt. Lucy dived into her '*quattro fromaggio*' and exclaimed over her mother's choice, replete with olives and sausage and with fresh herbs strewn over its surface. They decided to share.

Maria watched as Lucy happily replaced some of the energy she had spent in shopping.

She still had a treat in store for Lucy. The chestnut vendors were always set up on Ugo Bassi at this time of year. Maria felt sure the aroma of salted, roasting chestnuts would convince her daughter to sample the very Italian treat of hot chestnuts newly split apart with the heat from their roadside grills.

Lucy would have a hard time choosing between examining the crowds of elegant evening shoppers strolling the covered porticoes and checking out the fine goods in the windows of the big-name stores. The hustle and bustle of street life in Bologna would be something entirely new to Lucy. Her evening hours were spent at home or in friends' homes texting and listening to music or watching movies online.

Maria sipped her wine and sat back contentedly. She could not remember ever feeling so comfortable and content with her daughter. She sent a silent prayer of thanks aloft. I think we have made a new start, Lucy and I, and it's just in time.

Chapter Eight

❧

"Theresa, is that you?

Yup, it's me calling from sunny Italy.

Dad's away up north by now and I can't reach him, so I thought I'd bring you up to date with life here.

Oh, it's totally awesome! I know I didn't want to go at first but it's turning out to be a blast. I met this crazy good-looking cousin, or something, and he's been taking me about on his Vespa, a kind of motor scooter thing. We went to his university and he showed me around.

Bologna's pretty neat. It's an old place with really old buildings like churches and stuff and plazas they call piazzas with fountains and everything but the best part is the shops.

T'resa you would not believe the shoes they have here! They are actually hand-made and the colours !!! Wait till you see what Mom bought for me. They are beyond gorgeous and we only just started shopping.

No, that's not even the best part. You know the Twilight movies? Well, we are going to the town where they filmed the scenes from New Moon. I kid you not, sis!

My homies will just die when they see this. And that's not all! I am going to post a letter to Juliet in Verona soon. What? You missed *it? It's a movie about girls who have love problems. Oh, never mind, I'll rent it for you when I get home.*

Yeah, Mom's fine. She's not so bad when you get her away from the mall.

Listen, I'd better go. It costs a bomb to call trans-Atlantic, so they say.

If Dad calls you, be sure to tell him I'm having a great time.

If the school calls, tell them I'm never coming back! Ha! Ha! I wish!

Bye, T'resa!"

"Honest to God! Will that girl never grow up?"

Theresa's husband groaned and turned around, pulling the bed covers over his shoulders and muttering about people who didn't understand that late night calls should only be for emergency situations.

"That's the least of it," replied Theresa. "If she has woken the kids, I'll murder her when she gets back!"

Theresa slid out of bed and grabbed her warm robe. She could feel the chill as soon as her feet touched her cool slippers but there was no going back to sleep now. She was way too angry at her selfish young sister and she needed to check on the kids.

A quick look reassured her that all was quiet in the next bedroom but Theresa knew she was past the point of being able to snuggle into her husband's warm back and drift into sleep again. She tiptoed downstairs to the kitchen where she made a cup of chamomile tea in the hopes that it would calm her clenched stomach.

It's always the same with that girl, she thought. No concern for other people. She just does whatever she wants whenever it occurs to her. Did she even ask after her niece and nephew or apologize for waking us up in the middle of the night? Not a chance! She is totally focused on her own wants and needs and she has always been indulged by Mom and Dad. Look at this business right now. There she is off with Mom in the middle of the school term, on a free holiday in Italy with trips and treats galore and not one word of gratitude to her parents.

Would she stop to think that I am stuck here with work and kids and winter to cope with?

Oh, no, not Princess Lucy! She gets to swan off whether she deserves it or not. I thought the plan was that Mom and I would take the kids to Italy to meet their great-grandparents before they died. It would be wonderful to see the town where *il nonno* and *la nonna* were brought up. They have pictures of the area in their Toronto home and I always wanted to see it for myself.

But *I* am not the priority, that's obvious! Whatever Lucy wants, Lucy gets. There wasn't even any discussion about this trip beforehand. One minute I hear Dad's off to the frozen north for work and the next minute Lucy and Mom are flying to Italy for two weeks. Did anyone ask to see how *I* felt about it? Not damn likely! Out of sight out of mind for poor Theresa. Just keep soldiering on, Theresa. Your life is perfect, Theresa. Aren't you the lucky one! Huh!

When her thoughts reached this frantic pitch, Theresa could feel the bitterness burning her throat.

A few deep breaths and a sip of tea calmed her down. She was grateful that none of these thoughts had been spoken aloud or written out. She knew how damaging it would be for her husband and her parents to feel the anger she held against her sister. Nonetheless, it felt good to express some of her jealousy, even in silence. What she had thought wasn't all true of course. She was just reacting to the shock of being woken in the middle of the night by a thoughtless young sister.

Jealousy only hurt the one who held on to it, or so she had read in women's magazine articles, found mostly in the doctor's office. Theresa knew she was hurting herself with these angry feelings. Upstairs, asleep, were the reasons why her life was so much better than Lucy's. Family and love were the real rewards she had earned. Lucy had a long way to go to find a settled life and not a few personality disadvantages to overcome first.

Theresa knew deep down who was the really lucky sister; the one who had found her life already. In the daylight hours she would appreciate its benefits again.

She rinsed her cup, and climbed back upstairs. The sky had lightened. It would soon be time to start a new day, but first she would stroke the heads of her beautiful children and count her blessings.

Maria and Lucy arrived back at the villa late in the evening, happy but tired from the day's shopping adventures. Angela met them at the door with the news that a phone call had come for Maria and the caller had asked her to get in touch as soon as possible.

Maria's thoughts turned immediately to worrying about Theresa and the children, then to Paul.

What dire accidents might have happened to her husband in the far north?

While Lucy dragged herself upstairs with their parcels, Maria looked at the note Angela had copied down and recognized Anna's home number. She dialed quickly, relieved and guilty that she did not have a family emergency to deal with but also curious about Anna's urgent request.

"Hello, Anna. I just found out about your call. We've been out most of the day."

"Oh, I didn't mean to alarm you, Maria. Everything's fine at home. I talked to Theresa yesterday. She says the children are growing like weeds."

"Thanks for checking in with her, Anna. I've been so focused on Lucy lately that I have neglected my other daughter."

"I'm sure your time with Lucy will be productive, Maria. It's Susan and Jake I am calling about."

"I thought they were doing well. What's happened? I have been meaning to get in touch with Susan and now I am sorry I didn't do it sooner."

"Well, I'm afraid there have been some problems with Jake's health. He's recovering now but Susan has been advised not to fly back to Canada until he is in better shape."

"Oh, heavens, Anna! I had no idea. What can I do to help? Do you want me to go there and check out the situation?"

"Actually, I have a better idea but it needs a big favour from you and your family."

"I think I can speak for my family here, Anna. We'll do anything we can to help."

"I was hoping you would say that, Maria. I know it's presumptuous of me but I was wondering if Susan and Jake could take a train from Ferrera and spend a few days with you at the villa, just until they both feel stronger. It's been quite an ordeal for both of them at the clinic and I know Susan would really appreciate your support."

"Of course, Anna! That's a brilliant idea! A few days here with sunshine and good food, away from the hospital atmosphere, and they will both feel like new. I'll make all the arrangements and call Susan first thing tomorrow."

"Wonderful! Jake has had a complete checkup so you needn't worry about further complications for the immediate future."

"We'll take good care of them, Anna. Thank you for thinking of this. I'll keep in touch.

Bye for now."

"Goodnight Maria. Tell Lucy I am expecting great things from her."

With this enigmatic message ringing in her ears, Maria put

down her cell phone and leaned back in the chair to consider what she had just let herself in for. Her plans with Lucy would have to take a back seat until the situation with Susan and Jake could be resolved. There might be one day free before they arrived but there was a lot to be done beforehand. It might be necessary to call on Maurizio, or another of the young cousins, to chaperone Lucy for a couple of days. Maria felt a pang of regret. She had just begun to make headway with her Lucy project and now she would be unable to fully capitalize on that.

Still, surely Lucy would understand? She knew how close the Samba friends were and Susan had been Lucy's baby sitter when she was younger. Lucy used to talk about the dogs all the time and begged her parents for "a big cuddly dog to ride on" when she was small.

Maria reluctantly put thoughts of Lucy aside and concentrated on arrangements to accommodate her friends. Jake would need a bedroom on the ground floor. Fortunately, the big rambling old villa had plenty of space. There was an unused bedroom with a small bathroom nearby that could be cleaned and made cozy for the couple. Maria began to think of how to remove the bathroom door for wheelchair access.

The kitchen and outdoor area were on the same level. Jake could wheel himself outside easily and enjoy the view from the hilltop. The fresh air would revitalize his spirits and there was another advantage the villa offered, if Angela was willing to help out.

With her head full of new plans, Maria ran up the stairs to find a tray with tea and scones on the bed. Angela was such a dear person, she thought with a smile.

Lucy could be heard splashing and singing in the bath, so her grateful mother did not have to deliver the news of the unexpected visitors immediately. By the time Lucy emerged from the bathroom, her mother was fast asleep under the covers.

Susan and Jake arrived at the villa two days later. Lucy had been dispatched to visit San Gimignano with Maurizio and two teen friends who had also loved the New Moon movie, so Lucy was ecstatic to go with them wearing her new, sparkling sneakers and with her hair waved as a tribute to the style of Kristen Stewart, the actress who played Bella.

One glance at Susan's face told Maria everything she needed to know about the time her friends had spent in the clinic. There was an underlying tension there, and frown lines Maria had not noticed before. The normal Susan, capable, secure and confident had been supplanted by a frazzled, older woman whose clothes were crumpled and sweat-stained.

In contrast, Jake seemed quite relaxed. He was able to walk up the stone steps into the villa with a little assistance, and pushed his wheelchair before him into the bedroom, asking if he could take a nap right away as the journey had been tiring.

Susan saw Maria's inquiring look and as soon as the door had been closed behind her husband, she pulled Maria aside and started to talk.

"Don't be deceived by that, Maria, he's not as fit as he looks. It's partly the medication he's on and he's reacting to the reduced stress since leaving the clinic but it can't last long. I can see already that the symptoms are returning. Fatigue is only the first of them. His muscles are weaker, despite the good show he just put on for you, and I am pretty sure his eyesight is failing. He's masking the inevitable depression. I can't tell you what a relief it was to get your call and know we were safe with friends for a while."

Maria put her arms around Susan and felt her body trembling with emotion. This was not the Susan she had always known. She decided it was time for her to take over the mother-hen role that had been Susan's métier ever since she had known the Samba group.

"Now, my dear! Upstairs with you! You shall have a scented bath in my deep tub and I will unpack, air out, and wash your clothes while you relax. There will be a tray of sandwiches and a large glass of wine, (for medicinal purposes of course), waiting for you after the bath, and if you decide to sleep, just curl up in the bed. You won't be disturbed. This is a very quiet villa during the afternoons."

Maria escorted Susan up to her bedroom as she spoke, so there was no possible dissent from her plans. Susan was far from arguing. It sounded like an ideal way to spend an hour or two and, the truth was, she badly needed this kind of care. She allowed herself to be propelled into the bathroom while Maria continued to talk reassuringly and ran a hot bath whose fragrant steam made Susan's very bones melt with delight.

"Don't say one word more, Susan!" was Maria's parting warning. "I'll see you later and we can catch up then."

Maria ran back downstairs to prepare Susan's tray and to find Angela. The second part of her plan for Susan and Jake was about to be finalized. Maria had discovered that her cousin Angela was a qualified massage therapist who had a dedicated therapy room in the villa where she worked with a variety of clients and offered a wide range of healing techniques. Angela had assured Maria that a new meditation program she had been researching online had a number of proven benefits that could help Jake specifically. She reported to Maria that a recent study of 150 people with mild to moderate MS had demonstrated that massage, combined with a type of mindful meditation, had reduced symptoms of depression in 30% of the study's patients.

Angela was eager to try this technique with Jake, and Maria was sure Susan would approve.

By the time, Lucy arrived back at the villa, a dusky evening was following a glorious sunset.

Maria had spent an hour or two in the afternoon phoning showrooms and talking to her contacts in Milan to set up visits where she could select purchases from the summer and fall lines for the store in Canada. It had been comforting to resume her accustomed role as a professional businesswoman with an eye to fashion trends. Lately, all her attention had been devoted to Lucy's needs and now Susan and Jake required her help. She was surrounded with developments she had not expected on this trip but it felt good to be needed in the often-neglected role of mother and friend.

Lucy started to relate the events of her trip to San Gimignano before her mother could caution her to keep her voice down as their visitors were still resting nearby. She drew Lucy out to the terrace where the last of the light still tinted the clouds but Lucy hardly noticed so intent was she on impressing her mother with the wonders of the medieval town.

"Did you know there are eighteen really tall bell towers there? I don't remember them from the movie but they loom over everything like huge chimneys. Maurizio said they were warning towers to tell the people long ago when warring groups were advancing to the top of their hill.

We walked through all the twisty little streets and saw places where Alice and Bella drove the car then had to leave it when the road narrowed. We found the piazza with the fountain where all the actors gathered for the festival in the movie to celebrate the time they cast out the vampires. The DVD said they made hundreds of red cloaks for the actors and the townspeople to wear and, you won't believe it, Mom, I actually bought one in a tiny shop I found on a side street when I got lost for a minute."

Lucy dragged a bright-red cotton, hooded cape out of her purse and put it on, dancing around the terrace with sheer joy at the effect this prize would have when she got home to Canada.

Maria laughed to see her usually morose daughter so excited. Her feelings were contagious.

"Lucy, that's a wonderful souvenir but I have to ask you to quiet down a bit. We have visitors for a few days and one of them, your Uncle Jake, is not too well."

Lucy stopped her twirling and looked at her mother in surprise. "Is Auntie Susan here too?

When can I see her? The dogs can't be here I suppose. Wait! Does this mean we can't go to Verona now?"

The excitement drained out of Lucy's face at the prospect of a change of plans. Her mouth twisted into an ugly scowl and Maria felt a rising tide of annoyance as she watched the transformation. Lucy is not a child she said to herself. She should be able to put her own pleasure aside for the benefit of two people she loves.

For the first time since they had arrived in Italy, Maria forgot that her main purpose was to reconcile with Lucy. She would not have objected to Lucy's attitude toward her own mother, she was used to that, but when dear friends were affected she could not hold back her feelings of disappointment.

"Lucy!" she hissed, in a low tone, "I am shocked at your selfishness. You know how difficult it is for Susan and Jake. Can you deny them a little of our time when they have come here to recover from health problems?"

Lucy's eyebrows shot up when she heard her mother's tone of voice. She had almost forgotten how she sounded when a lecture was underway. She wanted to yell her response and justify her own point of view, but something in her mother's eyes turned the anger away. She plopped herself down on one of the mismatched wooden chairs and took a very deep breath before saying, "All right, I'm sorry, Mom. You have been so good to me on this holiday and I guess we both owe Auntie Susan some big favours."

Maria almost toppled backwards off her chair at this unusual turn of events. Who was this mature young woman who had suddenly appeared? Perhaps a day off on her own had done Lucy some good. Whatever the reason, it was wonderful to have Lucy on her side for once.

The two dark heads met together across the table and as night fell, they plotted out their strategy to look after Susan and Jake and to accomplish the objectives they had come to Italy to
fulfil.

Lucy didn't realize it yet, but her mother was mentally checking her own first objective off the list as partly on the way to being accomplished.

Chapter Nine

❦

The change in Susan was obvious after a day or two in the serene atmosphere of the villa.

She did not want to move from the terrace where she sat contemplating the incredible view down the slope full of olive trees and vines. The harvesting of grapes was now in full swing and every day brought local workers to gently detach the heavy plumes of rich red grapes and place them in wooden barrels in an old-fashioned, country way that spoke volumes about tradition and respect for the wine that would be produced in due time.

Susan watched their progress down the slope of the hill and thought about nothing. The rhythm of the work with breaks for lunch and coffee were sufficient to punctuate her days and she wanted nothing else.

Jake was being cared for by Angela and he seemed to respond well to her magical mix of body massage and meditation. Susan could hear the soothing music that indicated a therapy session was underway. The lovely sounds of waves or bird song seemed appropriate background for the relaxation therapy she was also experiencing.

Each day she could feel release from her muscles of the tension she was unaware she had been storing. She could only imagine the relief that Jake was gaining from the intensive work Angela was doing. Angela had announced that she wished to devote all her time to Jake for an initial period, as an experiment, to observe if the new program had the beneficial effects that seemed to be indicated by the study she had read about.

Susan could not comment on the medical results. She knew only that Jake slept deeply every night and woke happier every morning. She asked for no more than that for now.

Maria was content to leave her friend to the solace that sun and peace could supply. A family meal was planned for the weekend and Maria was busy helping the aunties to prepare the banquet of foods that were required. This involved copious large pots and pans being scoured and a bountiful supply of dishes and serving platters being retrieved from various parts of the kitchen and elsewhere in the villa, to the accompaniment of much chatter and laughter and debate about which person would be in charge of which signature dish.

Maria's role was restricted to chopping tomatoes and vegetables which arrived at the villa each morning from an ancient, battered car whose back seat was clearly used for produce rather than people. Maria unloaded these treasures for the aunties and marveled at the sheer beauty of the red and green peppers and bunches of spinach, parsley and celery that were kept cool until needed.

The kitchen was redolent with the scents of sauce preparation and pasta making and Maria inhaled memories of her childhood in every breath. She never seemed to have the skill or the time for such elaborate feasts at home in Canada. Her preferred method was a call to one of her favourite Italian restaurants, but that did not compare with this total immersion in the art and science of cooking. She watched and listened and thought a lot about her life choices while her hands performed the routine tasks she had been assigned.

In the late afternoons she made calls to Nova to check on progress at the store. It seemed so far away despite the excellent phone reception. It was hard to conjure up the busy mall in London with customers browsing through the racks and the sound of their distinctive carrier bags being popped open to receive a new, tissue-wrapped purchase.

The news was good, however. Nova reported that sales were steady and the cruise wear specials were drawing in their usual clientele plus some new, younger women who were planning ladies' fun weeks in exotic locations. Maria did not know whether to be pleased at this success, or sad that she was not needed at the helm.

She made other calls to Milan to save time when she eventually made the trip there. Her BlackBerry could receive photo files and although these pictures of current stock were useful, they could not supply the feel of texture and the detail of clothes' construction that was essential to a buyer.

Lucy, meantime, occupied herself upstairs at the villa with projects she would not discuss in any detail. To her mother's enquiry if she would be spending more time with Maurizio, Lucy responded in a dismissive tone, "Oh, his girlfriend was with us in San Gimignano. He'll be seeing her now."

Maria had to be content with this. She was glad Lucy had found something to keep her busy and that she was no longer complaining at the change of plans resulting from the arrival of Susan and Jake. Maria determined to reinstate the Verona trip for Lucy as soon as the weekend celebration had been observed.

❈

Sunday dawned bright and clear, promising a lovely day for eating outdoors at the huge wooden table on the terrace. Maria set out places and found extra chairs. She was unsure how many relatives were coming to welcome back the family from Canada, but she decided to use the space on both sides of the table rather than have to rush at the last minute.

In the kitchen, activities had risen to a fevered pitch. Maria could only marvel at the energy of the three sisters whose heads and hands seemed to be in five places at once. Maria helped to prepare *insalata* and stirred pots of redolent minestrone while platters of antipasto were sliced and laid out appetizingly. Some of the dishes defied Maria's description. She had to ask for names, even when she recognized some of the ingredients like osso buco and veal.

Every Italian dish she had ever tasted or heard about, was prepared, or in preparation, and the smells drew Lucy down from their bedroom.

"My Goodness!" she exclaimed, "what *is* this? I have never seen anything like this amount of food. Who's coming? The whole town?"

Maria chuckled. She had no idea who had been summoned but she knew both of them, as well as Susan and Jake, were honoured guests. The prime positions at the head of the table in the shade, were reserved for the titular heads of the entire family, *la nonna* and *il nonno*.

Maria had visited her elderly grandparents soon after she arrived at the villa, and had been amazed at the bright brown eyes peeping out through a network of wrinkles in the two faces, so alike now in old age that it was difficult to tell one from the other. The couple sat together with linked hands, the voluminous black skirts of nonna overlapping the wide, black pants of her husband, and Maria wondered if they walked together in the same way so as to support each other's bodies. They were cared for by Maria's oldest aunt, a retired nurse who devoted her time and energy to the old couple.

The thought occurred to Maria that this role could have fallen to her own mother, had she remained in the family home. How different her life has been in Canada, she mused.

What caused her to make such a huge change in her life? It

struck Maria that she had no answer to this question and she determined to ask her mother when she returned to Toronto.

All thoughts of home vanished when the family began to arrive. Maria and Lucy were greeted warmly by everyone, as were Susan and Jake. Much animated conversation ensued in both Italian and English. Switching between both languages was easy for most of the younger family members and Maria realized again what she had lost in not pursuing her language heritage.

As the laughter and teasing grew in volume the birds that usually spent the afternoons roosting on the old tiles of the villa's roofs, flew into the air protesting at the noise below that disturbed their peaceful slumbers.

Maria, Lucy and Susan were seated together with Maria's English-speaking cousins bracketing them on either side. Jake's chair was rolled into position near that of the family doctor who was anxious to know all the details about Jake's experiences in the Ferrera clinic.

As the rich red wine was poured into waiting glasses all conversation halted until toasts were made saluting first, the oldest family members, then the Canadian contingent, and lastly a young cousin who was about to be married.

As soon as the formalities were over, the eating began in earnest. Platters were passed around and even Lucy sampled a variety of dishes with ingredients she could not identify.

There was much laughter as the wine flowed, but every now and then the conversation became more general and the atmosphere was more serious. Lucy had been watching these episodes and listening intently.

"Mom!" she whispered, "I can hear words repeated often but I'm not sure who or what is being talked about. Is Napoli Naples? And what is the 'berlu scone' they all seem to be upset about?"

Maria wiped her mouth to conceal her amusement from Lucy and replied as discretely as possible, "You are right about Naples. There's another garbage strike at the moment and the whole place stinks to high heaven. The name Berlusconi refers to Italy's Prime Minister who is often in trouble for his behavior with underage party girls. They say they won't put up with his disgraceful attitude much longer."

"Ah, now I see what makes everyone throw their hands in the air. You have to be watching out for that here or you would get a black eye pretty quickly."

Maria agreed with her daughter. She listened again as the conversation turned to the topic of Pompeii. Lucy's attention was alerted by the familiar name. She had studied the wall paintings in Pompeii for an art project and tugged on her mother's arm until there was a break in the conversation that allowed her to interpret.

"It seems there has been a wall collapse in one of the houses. Silvio Berlusconi is being blamed for that too. Apparently not enough money has been assigned by the government to preserve the archaeological integrity of the structures."

"That's such a shame! I'd love to go there and see the town that was buried by the Vesuvius eruption."

"It's a wonderful place, caught in time, Lucy. We'll definitely add it to our list."

Susan had been listening in to Maria's comments. "There is so much to see in Italy. I am sorry I have not had the chance to explore some of the amazing sites here. This villa is incredible! Such a lovely location and it sits right into the hillside as if it had been here forever. Perhaps we can come back together some time and you can escort us, Maria?"

"I would love that, Susan. Listen! Would you like to come to Verona with Lucy and me? We are leaving early tomorrow. Would you be comfortable leaving Jake for a day?"

"Just look at him Maria! He is revelling in the weather, the food, Angela's treatments and the fabulous company. I doubt he would even notice I had gone."

"I know that's not true, Susan, but if you are sure, we'd love to have you with us."

Leaning in more closely, Maria added, "I think it's going to be a teenage dream day with the Romeo and Juliet connection. I'd be delighted to have some adult company."

"It's a deal then!" pronounced Susan, "but lunch is on me, if I can ever eat again after this extravaganza!"

After what seemed like hours, the wine carafes were emptied, the platters cleared of food and most of the family members were slowing down considerably. The grandparents had left much earlier in their daughter's care, and the remaining relatives were sipping strong coffees and venturing down the hill to inspect the quality of the grapes.

Lucy excused herself and went upstairs "to work" without explaining what she was doing there.

Maria turned to Susan and asked her to find out what Lucy was up to.

"She won't tell *me* what she's doing, probably so I can't object, but at least it's keeping her happy for the time being."

"I'll see what I can do tomorrow," replied Susan. "She might come clean to her old Aunt Susan and it would be a chance for me to thank you, in a very tiny way, for what you have done to rescue Jake and me."

"Please don't mention it, Susan. It was all Anna's doing and I have been delighted to be able to help you, for once."

Susan turned a solemn face to Maria and replied with unaccustomed seriousness, "I have never taken our Samba friendships for granted, Maria, but now I truly understand how important that connection can be for all of us."

The two women linked arms and smiled at each other in that special way when nothing more need be said.

It was time to check on Jake and hear how the afternoon had gone for him.

Chapter Ten

T he trio set off early for the taxi and train ride north to Verona. Maria knew the city was large with many interesting sights to see and it was the first opportunity for Lucy to explore a Roman-styled city with treasures to rival those of Florence and Rome itself.

Lucy had borrowed a leather backpack from Maurizio and pulled from it a guidebook for Verona she had found, nestled between cook books in the small library at the villa. She immersed herself in its pages as soon as they were settled in their seats on the fast train.

Maria and Susan were free to admire the passing scenery. Before long, Maria took the chance to ask Susan questions that had been on her mind.

"Stop me if this is too personal, Susan, but what do you see happening when you two get back home?"

"I can't tell for sure. He's so much better right now that I will search out someone in London or Toronto who can continue the type of therapy Angela is using. Beyond that we will have to wait and see what comes from the MS society's research projects. I think the public interest right across Canada will mean those projects will get a boost of money. I certainly hope so."

Maria considered, not for the first time, how difficult her friend's life must have been, living with a syndrome that affected everything and had an uncertain outcome. She decided the moment was right to ask Susan to reveal a confidence.

"Susan, this may be a question that crosses the line and if so, I apologize and withdraw it."

Susan's attention was now fully on her seat companion and the rumble of the train disappeared into the background as she grasped the younger woman's hand and said, "Ask away, Maria!"

"Well, you and Jake have been married for over 40 years. That's longer than anyone else in the Samba group. You've dealt with more problems than any of us but you are still together. What's your secret? "

Susan took a moment to consider her answer. Over the years she had occasions to ask herself whether staying, or leaving the marriage, would be best for her. Probably everyone in a long-term relationship had asked the same question. What she said now to Maria might have an effect on her marriage to Paul.

In the end, honesty was the only choice Susan could find.

"I don't know if there's a secret, Maria. Any long-term relationship has its ups and downs. With luck, you learn as you go, although I must be a slow learner as adjusting to married life took me far too many years."

"But, you had so much to deal with in health issues, Susan. I don't know how you coped."

"You have to remember, Jake was a fit, handsome young fellow when we first met. I was amazed that he wanted me. I was an up-tight, control freak even then and he was the free-wheeling catch of the college. They say people get together because they recognize something in the other that completes each of them in some important way. Maybe that's the answer.

I don't know, but at the start we had to fight many battles

before we reached the point where we accepted each other's differences and could appreciate them. Those were difficult but crucial times for us. The expression 'proved in the fire' comes to mind."

Susan chuckled at the memories but Maria was intent on her next question.

"When did Jake's illness begin to show itself?"

Susan had to think back to put a date on what had been a long slow progress.

"The early symptoms were not that easy to spot. Everyone, especially someone as active as Jake was, has an off day when they don't feel up to scratch. The occasional fatigue or muscle aches were ascribed to overuse while exercising. Jake played a fierce game of racquetball in those days and temporary injuries were not uncommon.

I think we were into our second decade before it became enough of a problem that we had to consult doctors."

"Did they diagnose MS right away?"

"Well, you wouldn't think so, perhaps, with such minor symptoms, but Jake had a very bad flu one winter and he noticed a loss of vision in his left eye. That was what drove him to the doctor. The doctor took a family history and when he found out Jake's mother came from Sweden originally, he suggested Jake might have MS and sent him for a battery of tests that confirmed what we feared."

"Why Sweden?"

"It's a northern country like Canada and that's where MS is most prevalent."

"What an unlucky set of circumstances. You must have been devastated, Susan."

"Truly, I was more concerned for my husband than for myself. The change for him was much more profound, in the long run."

"You have been such a strong supporter of Jake for all those years, Susan. How did you make it work?"

There was a long pause while Susan carefully considered, once more, what she would say.

"I think it's about friendship, Maria. If you start out as friends, no matter what intervenes in life, the friendship survives it all. Don't get me wrong, much of the change was hard for me to adjust to. I lost some vital parts of our life together along the way, but I was committed to Jake and in the end those cheesy marriage vows really do have an impact on your beliefs and your actions."

The two women sat quietly watching the scenery roll past and thinking about their respective marriages.

Susan was content with recent events and the restoration of her comfortable relationship with her husband.

Maria was absorbing everything Susan had revealed to her and thanking heaven she had not been challenged in such a way in her marriage to Paul. Their separations for work reasons had not resulted, so far, in a dilution of their feelings for each other. Maria determined that their friendship would be a priority as soon as she returned home and into Paul's arms.

Their quiet contemplation was shattered when Lucy declared loudly, "Verona is an awesome place! There's way too many churches and palaces of course, but it looks incredible. When we did Medieval Times in elementary school we should have come here. Verona had several castles, and fortified city walls right around the city back then and some are *still there*!"

Lucy moved forward to show her mother the map, unfolded from the back of the tourist guide.

"Look! It's a massive city! We'd need a week to see even half of it, but I think I've found the way to Juliet's house. We'll take a cab to the centre of the city and we'll probably cross the river to get there. The big piazza with the weird name is a good starting point but we'll have to walk for a bit from there. The road names change every few metres. The roads are not straight like in Canada. I think I can get us there if I keep an eye on the map. Did you see the movie about the letters to Juliet, Aunt Susan?"

"No, I haven't caught up with that one yet, Lucy. I have seen the Oscar winner of a few years ago, though. 'Shakespeare in Love' was the title and it told the story of the first performance of the play Romeo and Juliet in Shakespeare's England. I believe the story originally came from Italy and the playwright borrowed it for his own adaptation and that version has become world famous as a tragic play about star-crossed young lovers."

"I can't wait to see the place where you leave the letters for Juliet," Lucy sighed. I would write a letter myself but I haven't found a star-crossed love yet."

Both women silently thought Lucy was lucky to escape that fate but neither wanted to say so.

Lucy's 'big piazza with the weird name' turned out to be Piazza Bra which had nothing to do with women's underwear and more to do with the word *'braida'* meaning open space.

On the way there in the cab, all three of them almost had whiplash from the number of times they had to twist their heads to catch a glimpse of another tower, statue, monument or painted house. The bridges over the river Adige were no less spectacular but even these faded in comparison to the sight that met their eyes when the cab entered the Piazza Bra and they saw the massive structure that dominated the piazza.

Lucy was first out of the cab and stood in wonder as her mother paid the fare.

"Isn't that the Colosseum that's supposed to be in Rome?" she asked. "It never looked this big in the pictures I saw. Gladiators used to fight and die in there. What do they use it for now?"

"From what I can remember," suggested Maria, "it's called the Arena nowadays and large festivals or opera performances are held inside. Would you like to go in there, Lucy?"

Lucy shivered and replied in a quiet voice that she did not like the vibe after all the people suffered and died in there and she would rather find Juliet's house.

Maria and Susan exchanged looks but did not try to discourage her. Ancient buildings sometimes had that effect on people. Maria was learning more about her daughter's interests and sensitivities every day.

In spite of having a map to guide them, Lucy found it very difficult to track down Juliet's house.

She had already announced that they would not see the tomb of Juliet as it was in the opposite direction, but both Romeo's house and the *Casa di Guilietta* were reasonably close together and should be possibilities. Unfortunately, a combination of streets without anything approaching a safe sidewalk, and others that did not connect easily, resulted in confusion. While Maria and Susan were quite happy to wander in the general direction Lucy indicated, admiring whatever stately building or remarkable architecture presented itself along the way, Lucy grew more frustrated by the minute.

"I know it's near here. I remember the name Via Capello because it sounds like Juliet's cap.

It must be near here. I'll check around this corner."

By now, the sun was high in the sky and all three adventurers were glad to stumble into the Piazza delle Erbe where a sea of umbrellas covered market stalls and cafes could be found in the shade around the square. A refreshing lunch with salad, soft drinks and cool gelato soon restored their spirits and some careful inquiries by Maria pointed them in the correct direction for the elusive house of Juliet.

"The trouble is," Lucy grumbled, "these squares and streets are so close together that you can't see ahead to tell if you're going in the right direction. I prefer Canada where it's clear and open everywhere."

Maria did not argue. She flipped open the large umbrella she had acquired from a stall while Susan was paying for lunch, and under its sun protection they finally found Via Capello and through an archway on a side street the façade of a house with unique, three-lobed windows and a stone balcony could be glimpsed, whenever the crowds moved away for a moment.

Lucy was ecstatic. She searched the walls until she found the place where letters had been left for the team of Italian women who were employed to retrieve and answer them.

Lucy was very curious about the contents of these letters. She waited until a young woman approached with a folded paper in her hand and asked her what she had written. The young woman was an American tourist who had also seen the movie so the two girls made instant friends and talked endlessly about their favourite parts and the hazards of young love.

Maria and Susan took refuge against the ivy-covered wall to the left of Juliet's house and sat on the ground in the shade, sharing a bottle of mineral water Susan had been wise enough to purchase at the café.

Lucy and her new friend took photos of each other under Juliet's balcony and exchanged emails and phone numbers for future contact. They spent minutes in front of the simple bronze statue of Juliet in the courtyard discussing her height, clothes and hairstyle. Maria and Susan marveled at their instant friendship and overheard, with some relief, that the American girl had visited both Romeo's house and Juliet's tomb. She had advised Lucy to skip both of these locations as neither one compared to this site for dramatic effect.

❦

On the train back to Bologna, Lucy entertained her mother and Susan with the story Claire, the American, had told her. It seemed that Claire was older than she looked and at the advanced age of 21 she had fallen in love no less than three times, to the despair of her two sisters and her parents. Each romance had turned out badly, leaving Claire with uncertainty about her choices. Her banker father, who seemed to have escaped the recent downturn in the American economy, had chosen to send his daughter far away to Italy where she was, hopefully, out of reach of another suitor.

The last romance resulted in a broken heart because Claire's Romeo had spurned her for a younger, and according to Claire, an uglier, girl. This insult was not to be tolerated and Claire had taken her revenge. In the dead of night she had crept into her Romeo's apartment using the key he had once entrusted to her. With scissors in hand she shredded every piece of clothing she could find and left the pile on the floor of the living room where Romeo and his new love could not fail to discover it on their return from a night at the movies.

Claire was basking in a feeling of satisfaction about this act, when, to her horror, she found out that the debris of her former lover's clothing had been made into a viral video which was accompanied with a diatribe against Claire which assured she would never find another man to care for her.

Claire's letter to Juliet was a plea for reassurance that she had the right to her revenge act. The letter concluded with a request for advice on what she could do to recover her status as 'a nice girl'. Claire was determined to find the right guy and marry for life.

As Lucy approached the end of this story, the two senior women were doubled over with laughter, rocking the train carriage.

"Good luck with that!" burbled Susan.

"I can't believe she could be so naïve!" exclaimed Maria.

"But, she was a really nice person," insisted Lucy. "She just made some bad choices, I think."

"Well, let that be a warning to you, my girl!" chuckled Maria, with a wagging finger pointed at Lucy. "In this age of social media, nothing is secret and bad choices can follow you forever and into places you would never expect."

"Your mother is not joking, Lucy. It's quite true what she is saying. If you sleep around or even get a reputation for fooling around, you could find it difficult to correct that impression for many years to come."

Lucy looked pensive at this statement and finally asked, "I know it was easier to keep secrets in your day, Mom. There wasn't any internet to spy on you. Was it the same when your mother and father came to Canada? How did they meet and fall in love?"

"I was just thinking about that the other day, Lucy. I don't know the whole story about your grandparents, but I can tell you a part of it.

My mother learned to sew when she was a young girl. She trained with a seamstress in Bologna for several years then she was sent to New York to work for a cousin in the rag trade. She must have been skilled at her work because she ended up in a well-known American fashion house where she did alterations for clients who purchased their clothes from samples shown by showroom models. I remember my mother telling me how she got that job. She was told to select from a dozen bolts of cloth and return in two days with her own design of a size 2 sample suit for daywear."

"Wow! That was quite a test for a young girl."

"I think so too, Lucy. It was while she was working for the fashion house that she met and married my father. He was a long-distance driver who made deliveries of furs from Canada and when they found they were both from Italy the attraction was immediate."

"So it was a love-at-first-sight situation?"

"I think so Lucy."

"Well, that's what I would like. A first love that lasts forever just like you and Aunt Susan found."

"Don't think it's as easy as all that," warned Susan. "A good relationship has to be worked at all the time. You are lucky to have such good parents and grandparents, my girl, and don't you ever take them for granted. Just think

.... your talent, as well as your mother's, comes from the grandmother who worked so hard in fashion."

With this admonition to think about, silence descended on the carriage and all three thought of home and loved ones until each one fell asleep.

Chapter Eleven

A t the villa, the next day after the Verona trip dawned with a cloud-covered sky and light rain falling.

Maria decided to take the delayed trip north to Milan and she started out very early, leaving notes for Lucy and Susan.

She preferred to spend the day on her own in order to accomplish more. The previous contacts she had made by phone should make it easier to get around the busy city and she would hire a car and driver at the Milan train station. Bulk purchases would be sent on to Canada but any private purchases could be carried back to the train. She had a digital camera to photograph items that might be possible considerations later. This privilege was only granted to good customers and she was delighted to be able to do this kind of buying in person rather than by computer.

Maria took on her business persona as soon as she donned her smart navy suit for the day in Milan. Although she felt pleased with her progress toward connecting with Lucy, the familiarity of her work tasks was a comfort zone she could always retreat to.

She settled back in the express train and thought of the conversations of the day before. Lucy had, hopefully, heard some good advice along the way, from herself and Susan. Time would tell.

Before she put all domestic items out of her mind, she wondered if Susan would remember her promise to find out what Lucy was doing when she retreated upstairs for hours.

৩৫৩

Both Lucy and Susan slept late and awoke to the gray, rainy weather and to Maria's notes.

Lucy decided to have a lazy day and work on her project while her mother's prying eyes were otherwise engaged.

Susan thought she would cook omelettes and pancakes for everyone in the villa then spend time with Jake before his daily appointment with Angela.

Her agenda for later in the day included a heart to heart with Lucy. It was clear to Susan that Maria was deeply concerned about her younger daughter and if there was any way to get through to Lucy, it would be a chance to return the favour Maria had granted when she generously invited them to the villa and set up the program for Jake.

Susan suspected that Lucy still had a lingering respect for her, related to the time they had spent together when Maria was busy with her store and Susan had worked part-time at the lawyers' offices in London. Maria would drop Lucy off in the mornings and with the help of the dogs and Jake, Susan would entertain and educate the little girl until her father collected her at noon. Lucy relished the attention she got from the couple and both Susan and her husband loved the little girl who was like the child they never had.

Even after Lucy was of school age, they sometimes looked after her in the evenings when Paul was out of town and Maria was working the evening shift or involved in stock-taking chores.

The special contact lingered, and Susan often thought that Lucy behaved better in their house than she ever did at home.

The opportunity for quiet conversation arose after lunch, which was whole wheat pasta in a sauce so delicious that nothing more need be added to it. Lucy, Jake and Susan sat with Angela and the three aunties in the kitchen and talked together, with Angela's language help.

Lucy was delighted that she was always referred to as "*Bella Lucia.*" She knew it meant she was beautiful and the compliment was all the more welcome because it reminded her of the Twilight movie's main character, Bella.

Lucy followed Susan's lead and helped to wash up the lunch dishes. While their hands were immersed in water it was easy for Susan to ask the question that would start the discussion with Lucy.

"Listen, sweetheart, what's with you disappearing upstairs? Have you a secret boyfriend up there? A Romeo who ascends to the balcony?"

"That's not too likely, Aunt Susan! He would have to be Spiderman, to climb these walls and there's not much chance he wouldn't be seen by someone before he reached my window."

"Well then, what gives?"

Lucy put more force than was really necessary into dish drying while she considered this request. "Don't tell Mom, OK?"

"My lips are sealed."

"I have started painting and I don't want anyone to see my work until I've finished a series I'm working on."

"That's great news, Lucy! But why are you keeping it secret?"

"It's just that I haven't painted for years and I need to know I can do it well, before I share the pictures."

"Seems like a reasonable request. Can I ask what the paintings are about?"

"They're just views from the villa windows. I thought they

would be a good present for my grandparents. Years ago my dad took photographs of the area for my grandma and she has kept the photos on display in their house in Toronto. I thought they might like an update."

Susan stopped mopping up the tiled counter around the deep sink and turned her full attention on Lucy. "That's a wonderful idea, Lucy! Your grandparents will love the paintings and they will take pride of place alongside your father's photographs. How exciting for them to see talent come through in a new generation! They will be so proud, and so will your mother and father."

"Hmm! That depends on whether the paintings are any good at all!"

"I won't ask to see them yet, sweetheart, but I am sure they are brilliant since you have given your time and devotion to doing this for others. How do you feel about that?"

Lucy placed the last of the dishes on an open shelf and followed Susan to the patio doors where the rain could be seen falling steadily. They stood side by side looking out at the dripping foliage.

"I think it's been strange being here without my friends at school and the usual stuff I do with them. It's meant I have had more time to think."

"It looks like that thinking has been about other people in your life, Lucy. Am I right?"

"Yes, I suppose so."

"What conclusions have you come to, if I may ask?" Susan was afraid the conversation would end abruptly with Lucy stomping off upstairs again, so she was proceeding carefully.

"Well, I can't help thinking about family. This place is just heaving with family and it makes me aware of how people depend on each other."

"You mean like the way Angela has given up her time to help Jake?"

"Yeah, like that too. Mom just had to ask once and Angela stepped up to do a good turn for someone she didn't even know. *And* I am beginning to see what this holiday is all about. I didn't want to come at all at the start because I thought it was Mom's way of getting more work time and I was just dragged along since Pop was away."

"Have you changed your mind about that?"

"Well, Mom's working In Milan today but she has done plenty stuff with me all week and she really wants to understand me instead of always being on my case."

"I know your mother loves you very much, Lucy. She has been worried by the distance between you recently. She had to make some hard choices when you were young but she has more than made up for that, and now she hopes you will both be closer."

Lucy suddenly realized she was being put on the spot to make a statement she was not yet ready for. She turned around and looked Susan right in the eyes for the first time since their conversation had begun. "Thanks for talking to me, Auntie Susan. I need to get back to my paintings now. Please remember your promise."

Susan made the motion of zipping her lips and Lucy laughed out loud. It was something Susan had taught her when she was just little and they had to be especially quiet because Jake was asleep with the dogs by his side.

Lucy ran off, and Susan sighed. She had done what she could. Lucy was still a child in some ways but there were definite signs of maturity there.

🌢🌿🌢

When Maria arrived back at the villa, it was already night. She struggled out of the taxi with her parcels and bags and handed over a big tip when the driver went ahead of her and pulled the old handle that rang a bell inside the house.

Lucy and Susan opened the door at once and relieved Maria of her burdens, while asking her how her day had gone. Maria asked if she could sit down first before answering. She begged for a cup of coffee. She had not stopped to eat more than a snack in the Gucci Cafe since she wanted to get as much shopping done as possible in this day.

Lucy sprinted into the kitchen to fetch the coffee while Susan placed a cushion behind Maria and helped her out of the fitted jacket of her suit. Maria began to sense an urgency through her fatigue. What was going on? Both Lucy and Susan were positively humming with concealed energy. Were they really that anxious to find out if she had found any bargains in Milan?

"All right you two! What's up? You can't fool me. What have you done now?"

Lucy and Susan tried to look innocent but failed miserably. Susan was the first to recover her composure and asked, "Did you buy yourself any special occasion dresses in Milan, by any chance?"

"What? Why would I need special occasion dresses? You are not making sense Susan."

Lucy could not contain herself any longer and blurted out, "Mom! We had a phone call from Aunt Anna while you were out. We're all going to Scotland!"

Chapter Twelve

I t was some time before Maria could make out what Lucy was talking about. Her daughter insisted on dancing around the villa's kitchen waving a dishtowel above her head and shouting "Scotland! Scotland!" over, and over, at the top of her voice.

Susan was not much better. She was obviously pleased about something because her smile was huge and she was laughing so hard at Lucy's antics that she couldn't answer any of Maria's questions.

Just as Maria was getting worried that the pair had been drinking all the Lambrusco while she was away, they managed to calm themselves enough to sit down like rational creatures and speak sensibly.

"Sorry, Maria! We were just so excited at the news that we went a trifle overboard. We have been waiting behind the door for hours and we just exploded when we saw you."

"Fine, then! What news from Anna could possibly affect you two so much? Tell me for pity's sake!"

Lucy signalled to Susan to continue. She hardly trusted herself to speak clearly.

"Well, Anna called here to tell us that Bev and Alan have decided to get married."

Maria began to comprehend the reason behind the strange behavior she had witnessed.

"Really!" she exclaimed. "I had no idea they were planning this."

"It caught Anna by surprise too," agreed Susan. "Bev figured this trekking back and forth across the Atlantic would have to end sometime and they chose to make the relationship permanent."

"That sounds very practical, though not very romantic. What kind of wedding will it be and when?"

"Anna says we need to talk to Bev about the plans, but Bev has arranged the date for *this weekend* so we can all travel to Scotland from Italy and Anna will arrive from Canada."

"Are you serious? All the Sambas will be there? I can't believe a wedding can be organized so fast, even by Anna. You'd better get me some food. I think I'm imagining things!"

Susan and Lucy clattered dishes in the kitchen and with the aid of the microwave, managed to produce a scratch meal of reheated pasta and vegetables, and wedges of bread spread with the local butter.

The delay helped Maria come to terms with the change of plans and the food gave her the energy to summon up some enthusiasm for the work that was involved. Between mouthfuls of food she stated, "If this is going to happen so quickly, we need to change our flights home and you will have to contact the airlines too, Susan."

Susan nodded. "I've been thinking about that and wondering if Angela can come with us. I hate to cut Jake's therapy short when he is gaining so much strength. Do you think that's too much to ask, Maria?"

"I can't answer for Anna, but you know how generous she has been. We'll ask her as soon as possible. It all depends on where everyone is going to stay.'

Lucy was anxious to get to the important parts of the Scottish adventure. "What will I wear?

What will the weather be like? And will there be any guys there?"

Maria did not know where to start with Lucy's questions. "When we get more information from Bev I'll be able to tell you something, Lucy. At the moment I know less than you do. Let me finish this delicious food and I'll call Anna to get Bev's number."

"Let me do that, Maria, you have had enough to cope with for one day. Get off to bed and I'll sort out what needs to be done."

Maria gratefully accepted Susan's offer. Her head was still swirling with fashion trends for spring and summer 2011 and now this change of plans added a new layer of involvement. Hopefully, a good night's sleep would make everything seem more possible.

Lucy had to be content with this lack of information, but the issue of clothing was still foremost on her mind. She did not have a big choice among the casual items she had packed for Italy and she could not imagine that any of them would be suitable for a wedding event. She decided to run upstairs while her mother was talking to Aunt Susan so that she could arrange every bit of her clothing on top of the bed for inspection. She would have to be extremely creative to put something together for this emergency.

Susan borrowed Maria's cell phone and used the directory to access Anna's number in Canada.

"Hi Susan! I've been expecting your call. How did Maria take the news?"

"Well, she's a bit overwhelmed at the moment but Lucy's over the moon with excitement. She can't wait to get to Scotland."

"What can we do to make things easier for Maria?"

"If we can coordinate travel plans between us, Anna, then Maria can spend more time with Lucy before we leave here."

"We'll do that. How is everything going with Lucy?"

"I can really see a difference in her now. I think it was a good move to separate her from all the usual teen influences. She is much more considerate of her mother and Maria is more relaxed with Lucy, which helps enormously."

"I am so pleased to hear this. Is Lucy keeping busy?"

"Strange that you should ask that, Anna; she does have a project underway. I can't reveal the nature of it. You'll see it soon."

"Good! I had a little chat with Lucy before she left London. I asked her to give serious thought to her future career choices and mentioned I would help her in any way I can with the education aspects."

"Ah! I see! I wondered what was going on."

Susan tucked this information away for later consideration and turned to the topic of accommodations in Scotland. Anna had been thinking about this and thought she had a workable plan. Bev was already staying at Alan's with Eric, and James would join them there before the wedding, if possible. It could be a bit tight in the cottage at first until Bev and Alan left on their honeymoon to Skye. Kirsty would leave right after the wedding, accompanied by her relatives, to move into the charming Seniors Residence Home by the sea in Skye, to which she had always intended to retire. Bev and Alan intended to see Kirsty well settled there before they returned to the mainland.

Susan, Jake and Angela could join Anna in the McCaig farmhouse, which pleased Susan immensely as she had not yet had the chance to see the site of so much change in Anna's life.

She thought it was just like Anna to have included Angela without being asked. She had obviously realized how vital Angela's therapy had been to Jake.

Maria and Lucy could stay at a hotel in Oban although Anna thought they might prefer to split up and Lucy stay with Fiona in her wee cottage, giving the girl a close look at how Fiona had created a career out of less-than-the-best circumstances, while Maria could get to know Jeanette, George and baby Liam in their new Victorian home on the hill above the town.

"That sounds very organized, Anna. I couldn't have managed half as well. Thank you so very much for thinking of Jake that way. Every day with Angela's influence has such a positive effect on his health. One thing though, will there be enough space for us? I imagine Alina will stay with you at the farmhouse?"

There was a pregnant pause on the line and Susan immediately suspected something was very wrong.

"I didn't want to introduce this subject in the midst of all the wedding preparations, Susan, but I am glad you asked. Alina won't be joining us in Scotland.

She has had some sad news about her eyesight lately. It turns out that her mother had AMD, that's macular degeneration, and it has caught up with Alina."

"Good God, Anna! What a shock! I had no idea her sight was affected in any way."

"Well, neither did we! It's a long story for another time.

Don't mention it to anyone else, Susan. Alina has just started on a medical trial program for a new drug at the University's Research Centre. She can't interrupt the initial trial period at the moment, so I'll make Alina's excuses for now and we can work out the details when we get home to London. I really don't want to spoil Bev's special day with this news."

"Oh, I understand. Please tell her my thoughts and prayers are with her."

"I will certainly do that, Susan. Give Bev a call. She's on your time zone. I'll give you her cell number."

The call resumed with the practical details, but Susan could not get the shock about Alina's eyesight out of her mind. It seemed as if Susan was the recipient of secrets these days and it was not the most comfortable of positions to be in. Normally she would share worries with Jake but he was still in a fragile state of health and she was reluctant to burden him further.

In any case, it would be so good for the Samba friends to be together at such a happy occasion for Bev. Susan was looking forward to meeting Alan, about whom she had heard so much. She figured he had to be something very special to winkle Bev out of her solitary state after many years as a single mother.

These thoughts reminded her that contacting Bev was the next priority, so she settled down in the kitchen chair and dialed Bev's number.

"Hello! Bev here."

"Oh, it's so good to hear your voice, Bev, and to congratulate you on your wonderful news."

"Susan! I was just sitting here thinking about you. How is Jake? Anna says he will likely make it to the wedding and I couldn't be more pleased for both of you."

"I know. He's doing well now. It feels like we've come through a long dark tunnel and emerged into the daylight at last. Now what about *your* major excitement!

You should have seen Lucy dancing around the villa with a tea towel shouting that she was off to a wedding in Scotland! Honestly, Bev, how did you pull this together so fast?"

"It really wasn't as difficult as you might imagine, Susan. I suspect Kirsty was half-expecting to hear the news and had plans laid already. It all seemed to come together so easily. First of all, it won't be some fancy event with cake, church and reception dates scheduled months ahead. We'll be married in an Oban hotel by a minister who knows Kirsty's family and the same hotel will cater a meal for us. I don't want a lot of fuss and bother. It will be a simple ceremony but I can't tell you how happy I am my Samba friends will be there.

Alan's family from Skye will be the majority of the guests and I don't know how many of them will turn up on the day. Oh, that reminds me, Susan! It's the custom here to hold a ceilidh, a kind of dance and music party, after the ceremony, so tell Lucy to bring her dancing shoes. It will be a wild night if I know anything about these islanders."

"It sounds wonderful, Bev! I can't wait to meet Alan."

"Well, he's not a Canadian, Susan. It takes time to get to know him, but I can assure you, it's time well spent. He is a lovely man in so many ways and he is so good for my boys."

"Your voice changes when you speak of him, Bev. That's a fine recommendation as far as I'm concerned."

"Thanks Susan. You'll love him too."

"Oh, my dear girl, I didn't mean to take up your time this way. You must have plenty to do, despite what you say. We'll be with you the day before the wedding, if at all possible. Much love from all here. Goodbye for now, Beverley."

Susan could feel tears gathering after that emotional talk with Bev. It was amazing to think that the Sambas would have a wedding to celebrate. Kudos to Bev and Alan for taking the plunge

later in life. It was a brave move for Bev to settle in a new place, in a new country and in a very different lifestyle, but it was what she wanted, with the man she wanted, and that was a very good start, as far as Susan was concerned.

Chapter Thirteen

※❦※

Maria's plan to flop into bed had to be set aside as soon as she saw Lucy's entire travel wardrobe spread across their bed.

"Oh, there you are, Mom! Please help me decide what to wear to this wedding. I can't see any prospects in this rubbish."

"There's nothing wrong with your clothes, Lucy, but if *you* can't find a suitable outfit, with your creative talents, I don't know what the rest of us will do."

"It's no joke, Mom! I can't turn up at a wedding in distressed jeggings and these glitter sneakers. Did you bring any scarves or belts or stuff from Milan in those carrier bags? I need some inspiration."

Maria looked at Lucy's slim jeans with the ripped sections over the knees and refrained from saying 'I told you so'. She had never liked the style, preferring something more feminine, but she knew better than to suggest that to her daughter.

"It will be November when we get there, Lucy, and Scotland is farther north than south-west Ontario. I don't think you will need anything too light or floating, for a start, but I agree that those jeans won't do."

With some reluctance, Maria reached for one of the bags she had brought back with her. The items inside had been intended for Theresa as a compensation for missing the holiday. The beautiful, full, wool skirt in a subtle plaid and the soft leather jacket, fitted to the waist, would suit either one of her daughters in colouring and size. She would just have to find something even more gorgeous in Toronto for Theresa.

"Well, Lucy, I didn't buy any accessories on this trip. I always get a huge selection at The Clothing Show in Toronto in the fall, but I do have this lovely outfit. Do you think it's your style, Lucy?"

Maria stepped back and allowed Lucy to take the clothes out of the designer bag. The prestigious label was not lost on Lucy but she pretended to be uninterested in the source while she held the skirt and jacket against her and examined the effect in the big old dresser mirror.

"Obviously, it's something quite different for me but I think it might suit the occasion quite well," she conceded in an understated way.

Inside Lucy was jumping for joy. She knew her mother must have dropped a bundle of cash on this fine wool and ultra-soft, wine-coloured leather. She began to plan what she would wear underneath the jacket; something jazzy perhaps for the unexpected contrast if, or when, the jacket would be removed.

Maria knew the problem was solved as soon as Lucy fell silent and contemplated the clothes with that look of concentration that indicated her creative mind was at work.

Finally, she turned to Maria and said, "I think this will do very nicely. It's really beautiful, Mom. Thank you so much. Now, what are *you* going to wear to the wedding?"

A heated discussion ensued. Maria stated she was happy with the navy business suit she had worn to Milan. Lucy insisted it needed some sparkle for a special occasion and produced an emerald-green, silky, tank-style top with shoulder details that Maria instantly recognized as something from her own closet.

"Where did you get that young lady?" she asked, accusingly.

"You know where, Mom! I thought it might just come in handy on our trip and see how right I was! It will lift that suit into another dimension."

Maria couldn't argue with her daughter. The top was perfect.

Exhaustion overcame Maria all at once. She had just enough energy left to undress while Lucy hung up her clothes. As soon as the bed was cleared she pulled a night-dress out from under her pillow and was asleep before Lucy emerged from the washroom and put out the light.

࿇

Susan insisted on a fashion show the next morning. She wanted to see what she was up against. Taking the role of poor relation was not what she wanted. There were few members of Bev's family attending this wedding and it was incumbent on the Sambas to support the Canadian team.

Susan's packing for Italy had not included any dressy outfits. She had rightly assumed Jake would not be feeling like nights on the town after his days at the clinic.

The only spot of comfort Susan could derive, after she had surveyed the remaining sad candidates hanging in the wardrobe in the villa's bedroom she shared with Jake, was that she had the assistance of two of the most fashionable and smart women she knew. If they couldn't come up with something appropriate for her to wear, it was a hopeless cause, indeed.

Saying nothing of this, she sat back and watched the parade of Maria and Lucy's chosen outfits on the terrace. Rain had brought a cold snap overnight and the leaves on the vine above the table had crisped and turned yellow. Maria's navy suit with a draped back panel, brought her dark hair and the touch of emerald at the neck into sharp relief against the golden leaves.

She had found a tiny fur-trimmed hair attachment that she perched to the side of her elegant chignon and the effect was glamorous and yet understated. Maria would be a credit to Bev for certain.

Lucy pranced onto the terrace wearing a spectacular wool skirt that swirled around her hips with every movement, and made Lucy look so sophisticated that it was easy for Susan to see a job as a runway model in her future. She had paired the skirt with knee-length brown leather boots with high wedge heels. The maroon leather jacket that hugged her curves was the perfect finishing touch and Lucy had left the jacket open to show a glimpse of an amber-coloured, satin top that picked up a similar thread in the plaid skirt and brought out the highlights in her shoulder-length hair.

"Heaven help me!" thought Susan, "I can't compete with this pair of fashionistas! And I can't borrow anything from them. I am much closer to a fourteen while both of them are size ten or less."

Maria saw the expression on Susan's face and recognized a mix of pleasure and perplexity.

She took Susan's hand and suggested a trip into Bologna to purchase something for Jake and Susan to wear. "It will be our last chance to pick up items before we leave for Scotland, Susan.

Lucy and I will be glad of the opportunity. Please come!"

"Oh, Maria, I can't afford clothes at the moment. I owe Anna for expenses already and, frankly, there's not much left in the pot after the plane tickets are bought."

"Now, don't worry about all that. This is a very special event and I insist we all travel in style.

I can get discounts in Bologna and there are wonderful places to get excellent bargains. I will kit you out head to foot, Susan, and we'll figure out something appropriate for Jake too. It will be my pleasure to do this. Now don't dare protest!"

Maria could see the objections colour Susan's face and she cut them off before Susan could start.

"Sambas stick together, remember? I have always wanted to buy something for you, Susan, and this is the right time, for sure. Please?"

Susan could hardly refuse Maria's generosity when she used that wheedling voice. Her lovely face showed how sincere she was and Susan felt a feeling of relief that she would not have to worry about this part of the wedding plans. She found a smile somewhere and pulled Maria into a firm embrace so that she did not have to answer. Her throat was restricted by the emotions she felt for her friend.

"That's settled then!" declared Maria. "We'll all spend the day in Bologna tomorrow and see what we can find. It'll be fun to show you around, Susan. Lucy and I have our favourite places already."

Susan accepted the inevitable and listened as Maria warned Lucy not to prance about on the uneven paving stones in those boots. "I want you fit to carry our cases when we fly to Scotland, Lucy. We will be far too elegant for such tasks. Just wait and see."

❦

"Nova, it's Maria. I'm still in Italy."

"Oh now, it's great to hear your voice, Maria. When are you coming home?"

"That's the problem, Nova. I won't be home for a few more days yet. We have been invited to a friend's wedding in Scotland this week and I just have to go."

"Surely! That's the thing to do! You have no worries here, at all. Business is booming at the store. I've unpacked all the reserve boxes in the back and the cruise wear has been a big hit. The weather

people are saying it's to be a bad winter and I think everyone is planning on escaping it as soon as they can."

"That's wonderful news, Nova. I am really proud of the way you have coped with everything. I gave you very little notice, you know."

"Not at all, Maria! You work too hard and I am delighted to be able to give you a break. What were the styles like in Italy? Did you buy anything special for spring and summer?"

"Well. It's all the pale tones we saw last year with a few splashes of colour like orange, and some blue and white nautical lines for spring, as usual. There's a new rosy-magenta appearing in some of the couture lines and lighter versions of the popular animal prints."

"Those should work well with our clients' needs. I'll start thinking about new displays for you to approve, Maria."

"You are a treasure, Nova. I can't thank you enough. I haven't had one minute of worry about the store, knowing you were in charge."

"Indeed, that's kind of you to say. I have enjoyed the responsibility but you should know that you are not forgotten. Several of your regulars have been in here asking about dress designs for Christmas events. I assured them you were working on their behalf in Italy, but they insist on seeing the Boss Lady herself."

"Keep them happy with the photos I will send on to you, Nova. I found some beautiful dresses In Milan which are being sent to you by air. I'll send notes about who would suit each item and you can contact them directly."

"And that is why you are the Boss, Maria! That kind of thinking makes all the difference in this business."

"Thank you again, Nova. I'll be in touch soon."

"You take your time and enjoy that wedding. Don't they say 'carpe diem' in Italy?"

"You are right, Nova! I'll try to seize the day and slow down once I get home. I've been enjoying the slower pace here for sure."

"Take care of yourself, now. Bye for now, and have a drink of wine for me."

. . .

Maria had to smile at Nova's advice. She really should be thinking about starting packing but perhaps Nova was right about enjoying the moments of life. She turned to the bedroom window and decided to pick up a jacket so she could take that glass of wine out to the terrace and sip it while she watched the sun set. She promised herself she would think of nothing serious, other than the incredible view from the hilltop. She considered that a few minutes counting her blessings would not qualify as serious thinking.

Chapter Fourteen

⁂

"Theresa! What the hell is wrong with you? You look shattered. Are the kids alright?"

Joe quickly shrugged out of his work clothes and heavy boots leaving the dusty pile just inside the front door. He knew something was seriously wrong when his wife ignored the mess he had left. She walked slowly into the family room ahead of him and dropped down on the sofa as if the weight of the world was on her shoulders.

Now Joe was even more concerned. He cast his mind around to see if Theresa had a doctor's appointment scheduled for herself, or the children, but he couldn't recall any changes to the regular calendar. Probably not trouble with the children's health, then.

What if something had happened to Maria or Paul? Paul was so far away and Maria was out of touch for part of the day due to the time difference in Europe. Bad news about either one of her parents could easily create the kind of depression he was witnessing in Theresa right now.

Joe could wait no longer. "Theresa, Honey, you have to tell me! I'm going crazy here, imagining the worst."

Theresa's tears flooded down her cheeks at this statement

and she threw herself into Joe's arms and sobbed her heart out. "I've been fired!" she said into Joe's sweater.

"What did you say? I can't make it out between sobs. What's happened?"

Theresa managed to lift her head a fraction and repeated in a rush, "I've been fired, Joe. I haven't enough seniority at the office since I took time off for the babies and they are cutting staff because of the economy and they can't promise me I'll get my job back any time soon."

The sobs started again as soon as she had unloaded this news.

Joe could only pat her back as soothingly as he could while his mind raced.

This would mean financial difficulties for the family. Luckily he had a secure job for the winter months, working on construction at a mall in the city, so, if they were careful they could survive until Theresa found more part-time work. Still, it would mean changes to their lifestyle in the short term.

The idea that Theresa might not find more work was not to be considered. They could just manage the mortgage and the babysitter when one and a half salaries were coming in every month but his pay would not support all four of them without digging into the minimum savings they had in the bank. He decided to downplay the worst-case scenario and provide some comfort to his stricken wife.

"Look, Love, it's not your fault! Don't cry! We'll work something out. As long as we are all well, nothing else matters. You know that's what your father always tells you."

Fresh sobs met this reassuring statement, to Joe's surprise.

"That's *another* thing; I miss my Dad! He's been gone for nearly three weeks and I want to talk to him about this."

"Can't you call him?" Joe knew better than to feel rejected by his wife's attachment to her father. There was a bond between them that had been obvious from the first time Joe had entered their home when Theresa was just a teenager.

"I can't reach him! He's so far north it takes a satellite exactly in place over their heads to get a signal and he has called while we've been out. Mom is far too busy with Lucy to call very often and that's *another* thing .... Lucy has called again and she is just rubbing my nose in the fact that Mom and she are having a grand old time with Aunt Susan and the family in Italy and <u>now</u> she tells me they are not coming home right away! They're going on to Scotland for a wedding, would you believe!"

Joe had taken in only one quarter of this latest rant but he did notice indignation had taken over from despair in Theresa's voice. He was not sure this was an improvement, however.

"Now, now, Honey, you promised you wouldn't let jealousy spoil your relationship with your family."

Theresa reacted violently to this perceived accusation by pushing her husband away and swiping the tears off her cheeks while exclaiming, "That's just not fair, Joe! Why am I always being left out? Lucy gets all the attention and I'm the one who works hard for my family."

Joe recognized that a new tactic was required at this juncture if calmer waters were to be found.

"You're right! You're right, Honey! I didn't mean to suggest you don't deserve the best of everything. I only wish I could give you all the things you deserve right now but times are hard and it will be a while until I can get a site manager's job then we'll do all the travel and family visiting you want. Just be patient with me."

Theresa recognized at once that she was being grossly unfair to complain to her husband. Joe worked all the hours he could get, to provide for their family and she was displaying the very selfishness she accused Lucy of when she let her baser feelings run wild like this. She made a quick mental shift and pulled herself together, back to the mature Theresa, Joe had every right to expect in his wife.

"Joe, I am so sorry! It's been a rotten day and I felt overwhelmed for a minute. None of this is your fault. We'll manage somehow and I know Mom has been a great support for me. This time with Lucy is something she needed and if it works out, we will all benefit."

Theresa gave Joe a watery smile and sat up straight. She was a married woman with responsibilities and children to care for and she needed to act like it.

"I had better go upstairs and warn the babysitter that she is out of a job too. It will be good for me to spend more time with our kids, Joe. There's always a silver lining in every cloud, or so they say.

Get washed up for supper. There's a casserole in the oven and the kids will be ready to eat.

I've been down in the dumps for long enough. Don't you worry! Normal service will resume immediately!"

Joe watched his wife skip up the stairs and relaxed. When Theresa could make a joke he knew everything was fine again. The stormy weather had passed.

❦

Anna watched the wind strip leaves from the trees in her backyard. The season was turning from mild autumn to brisk November. Fall was a sad time for many. The end of the year loomed and winter was fast approaching.

It had been a good year for the A Plus business she shared with Alina, but changes were inevitable on that front now. Alina's deteriorating eyesight would mean the work she did designing knitwear would be much more difficult for her.

Anna thought of the dress Alina was working on for Bev's wedding. It was the most beautiful garment Anna had ever seen and suited Bev's simple style perfectly. The top layer was a lacy overdress, like a cobweb, crocheted by hand. It was designed to float over a simple, long-sleeved, blue satin gown that brushed the floor but had no train or extra decoration. The drama was in the delicate lacy structure with wide sleeves that would drape perfectly when Bev held her bouquet. Anna had insisted that the drop crystals scattered around the top of the overdress could not be sewn on by Alina herself. This task had been taken on by a trusted worker, against Alina's protests, of course, but Anna had seen the eye fatigue and headache that resulted when her friend worked too long or too closely.

The gown was almost finished, and Anna would take the box on the plane with her to Scotland.

She sighed. The rising wind outdoors absorbed the small sound. It would be sad to go back to their Scottish home without her partner. Alina hated to miss such a special occasion but her doctors had advised against travel at this point in her treatment.

Anna had not intended to return to Scotland so soon. She and Alina were planning to celebrate Christmas in Canada this year with their Samba friends and their families, but with everyone travelling around the world, it seemed, the prospects of that happening were not so great at the moment. Even Philip, Anna's newly-discovered half-brother, was not able to attend the wedding on such short notice. He had visited Simon and his family in Alberta in the summer, when Anna and Alina were in Scotland, and was now in Egypt supervising a building project for which his firm supplied the lead architects.

We are all scattered to the winds, Anna thought.

She shook herself out of this morose attitude and decided to make a pot of tea and re-focus her thoughts. There was a lot to do before she crossed the Atlantic again. She wanted to invite the specialists from The Canadian National Institute for the Blind to check over the house before she left. Simple changes would make it easier for Alina to cope around the house, should she need them in the future. It was best to be proactive in these situations. They would hope for the best with Alina's macular degeneration treatment but it was always better to be prepared for the worst, as her mother used to say.

Thinking of her mother brought another of her old sayings to mind. When she got older, her mother would say, in a Scottish accent that Anna rarely heard; "Auld age never comes its lane."

Anna puzzled over this until she finally asked her mother to translate.

Many years later, Anna understood the meaning. The illnesses of old age are inevitable.

As she thought of Alina and Jake and the sad demise of Philip's mother from dementia, she also acknowledged the good health of Maria, Susan, Bev and herself.

"I won't take my health or anything else for granted," she informed the kettle as she poured the boiling water over teabags in the heated pot. "I have so much to be thankful for and plenty to look forward to."

She heard Alina's key in the front door and went to meet her with a smile.

"Just in time for a hot cup of tea, my dear. How was your day?"

Paul had finally got a satellite connection to his wife's cell phone in Italy. They had a long chat and Maria filled in the events both of the past two weeks and the coming weekend in Scotland.

Paul was pleased to hear the time with Lucy was productive. Maria seemed very hopeful that fences had been mended and the future looked brighter as far as her relationship with their younger daughter was concerned.

Paul was also relieved to hear the more relaxed tone in his wife's voice. It was easier for an observer to see how stressed she had become of late and the change was very welcome to him. It did not appear that Maria was overly anxious to return to work. This fact alone, reassured Paul that some significant changes had occurred in his wife as well as in his daughter.

He replied to Maria's questions about his expedition in vague terms, suggesting that the photographs would describe the Arctic environment far better than mere words could.

The team had been alarmed by the conditions they found. Those experts who travelled with them noted the deterioration in the permafrost that signified rapid temperature increases.

The news was not good, but Canadian Geographic would be pleased with the series of articles the photographs would illustrate. Paul was confident he would return in a month or so to document further changes. The connection with the prestigious magazine was exactly what he had hoped for.

Meantime, he needed to make the slow trip back to South-western Ontario, weather systems permitting, of course. He would check in at home and change into lighter clothing, then see Theresa and Joe and the children.

Maria's plan had included a couple of days in Toronto on the way home with time to see her parents. Paul thought it would be a good opportunity to surprise Maria and Lucy. If Theresa could get away from work, they could travel together to the airport and meet the pair from the plane.

He thought longingly of seeing his wife again. Although they were used to such work-related separations, the reunions were worth the loneliness. They both found it was like meeting for the first time without the uncertainty of wondering whether or not the affair would last.

His mind wandered back to one of their first dates. They had gone to see the movie, 'West Side Story', and had been captivated by the music, the dance, and the modern retelling of the old Romeo and Juliet story. It had been one of their favourites ever since.

Paul smiled as he realized how that iconic story still affected him. His iPod, a constant companion in leisure hours in the north, held the tune 'Maria'. Whenever he heard the song's plaintive repetition of the name, he couldn't help a surge of longing for *his* Maria. In some ways, they were still that young couple, without the sad ending Paul hastened to add. It was about time he introduced the movie to Lucy. She was just the right age to appreciate the teenage angst.

Paul determined to take his family to one of the fancy airport hotels for a couple of nights. He would book two rooms, re-establish their family connections, and they would visit Maria's parents without the stress for the older couple of coping with a family invasion.

Paul's plans were interrupted by a report from the weather monitors. A storm system was bearing down on them from the west and north. If they wanted to vacate the research station they would have to pack up the equipment, summon a land vehicle to transport them to the nearest airstrip and start the long journey home.

Chapter Fifteen

✿❀✿

P acking seemed to be taking a long time. Maria had extra items of clothing to find room for, but so did everyone else in the group. Only Angela was ready to leave with just one suitcase.

Maria knew that suitcase would contain a fine merino wool outfit for the wedding. She had not needed to ask Angela if she required some new clothes. Any Italian woman of Angela's age had fabulous dressy clothes. She might spend working hours in a washable and practical uniform, but Maria knew for certain that Angela would be dressed like an Italian princess for the wedding.

Susan and Jake were also ready to go. Susan's new clothes were wrapped in tissue and enclosed in a plastic zipped bag, supplied by Maria. The dress and jacket, chosen in Bologna, were a perfect complement to Susan's new hairstyle. It had been a delicate contrivance to manoeuvre Susan into a hairstylist's salon in Bologna, on the pretext that both Maria and Lucy needed a trim anyway. While Lucy's locks were receiving the trim and a conditioning treatment to eliminate split ends, Maria had a word with the stylist and suggested a more youthful cut for Susan's fine, iron-grey hair. A few expert snips and the transformation was complete.

Each woman left the salon with the spring in her step that only a refreshed hair style can achieve.

The dress Maria chose for Susan was a fitted, silver-grey jersey with a deep V neckline and an almost Empire waist that emphasized Susan's curves beautifully. The skirt flared over the hips and ended just below Susan's knees. The matching jacket was black, piped in silver, and with unique silver buttons.

New shoes were a necessity, Maria had stated, and by this point Susan was too bemused to object further. A search among the stores found, with Lucy's help, a pair of grey and black suede court shoes with a block heel that Maria assured Susan would be comfortable under any circumstances, for a few hours at least.

Susan had spent most of a day on the phone with her own, and Maria's, airline etickets spread out on the kitchen table and copious notes about dates and times scattered here and there. The easiest way to accomplish the change of tickets turned out to be the expensive phone connection back to Canada so that Anna's London, Ontario, travel agent could supply the information online to an international agent and work out the changes at the best possible cost.

Eventually they acquired the five tickets to Glasgow on the same plane, and two returns to Toronto for Lucy and Maria. Anna had advised Susan and Jake to stay on for a few days at the farmhouse with her so that Angela could continue Jake's therapy. This plan would allow Jake's sister to drive north to Canada with their dogs so the reunion at home would be complete. Jake's sister, Rena, was anxious to see her brother's progress and would stay with the couple for another week or so provided the weather was not too bad for the drive back to Florida.

It took quite a lot of effort to pack the cases Lucy and Maria had arrived at the villa with. There were the new outfits, shoes and underwear that had been purchased, in addition to various tourist maps, pamphlets and brochures that Lucy insisted on saving.

Maria had almost closed her case and re-packed the carry-on bag for the fifth time, when Lucy appeared from the washroom with a strange expression on her face.

"Mom?" she began, and Maria knew there was trouble.

"What's up, Lucy?"

"Well, I was hoping to keep this a secret but I guess I forgot to think about the size."

"Size of what?" Maria's heart sank. Lucy had bought something heavy or huge, and now there would be no space to pack it.

"You see, I wanted to try painting again, so I found canvas and paints in San Gimignano, in a tiny art shop beside the little shop where I bought the red cloak? I've been painting pictures for a while now and I think I need to take them back to Canada."

"Lucy, that's wonderful! Can I see them?"

Lucy disappeared back to the washroom closet and emerged in a few moments with a bundle wrapped in an old shirt.

"I've been keeping these away from you, under the bed." Lucy carefully placed the bundle in her mother's hands.

"Now, don't expect too much, Mom. I haven't painted for years and I had to work at it for a while before I got what I wanted."

Maria unwrapped the six canvases and laid them on top of the bed.

There was complete silence in the room while Lucy waited anxiously for her mother's verdict.

Maria was stunned by what she saw.

Finally, when she could speak again, she declared, "Lucy, these are incredibly good. You must have been painting from this room and other rooms on this floor. The angle gives you such a long perspective, right down the hillside towards

Bologna far in the distance. You have caught the whole feel and atmosphere of the villa perfectly."

Maria paused again, "Is this me watching the sunset?"

"Yeah, that's the last one I did. It was very difficult to capture all the colours but I think it worked out all right."

"The paintings are more than all right, Lucy. This is very good work. I can't wait for your father to see them."

"Now, that could be another problem, Mom. I painted them for Nonna and Nonni's home in Toronto."

"But that's a wonderful, generous idea! You know they will be so grateful to have these.

It's many years since they made the trip to Italy and this will remind them of Nonna's childhood here."

"Do you really think so?" Lucy's tone revealed her as a little girl who still needed approval. More than anything else she said, this tone spoke volumes to her mother.

Maria ran to the other side of the bed and caught her daughter in a huge bear hug that squished all the air out of Lucy's lungs. "I tell you the paintings are *amazing* and your grandparents will be ecstatic, not to mention your father, Lucy. He will be so proud of you, but not one bit more than I am at this minute!"

Lucy hugged her mother back, then disentangled herself and whispered, "But how do we get these back to Canada?"

Maria looked again at the canvases. They were all the same size measuring about 1.5 metres square. Their cases were out of the question, so special packing would have to be found.

"We will take them on board the planes with us, Lucy, we'll find a post office or stationery store to supply a rigid box. Maybe Maurizio will know where to go for that. What about paints and brushes?"

"Oh, don't bother with those. The paints are almost finished and the brushes can stay here. If we can get the paintings home in one piece I will be happy. The proper framing and matting can be done in Toronto once Nonna sees them and tells me what she would like."

"In a way, I wish we were going home right now, Lucy." Lucy understood her mother's declaration. So much had happened in Italy and there was so much to tell her father and Theresa but there were other considerations as far as she was concerned.

"No way am I going to miss that ceilidh, Mom. I plan to be the belle of the ball, besides the bride, of course!" she added hastily.

Maria never noticed. She was gazing at the painting of herself alone on the terrace with the glass of wine in her hand. There was something very solitary and lonely about the figure; a kind of vulnerability that Lucy had caught perfectly. I am not the tough business woman I thought I was, she concluded. Lucy is not the only one who has changed here. We came just in time for me to learn a few very important lessons before it was too late.

❦

Despite all the last-minute problems, they were finally ready to go. Family members had wandered in and out the day before to wish the travellers well, on the next stage of their journey.

Maria and Angela had decided to take two taxis to the airport as the wheel chair and the luggage took up a lot of space. The bags were stacked outside and only the hand luggage and Lucy's paintings were left in the kitchen.

The three aunties stood together in front of the door like a defensive guard blocking their exit. A long speech began which Angela translated for Lucy. Her mother already understood what had been said and she looked surprised.

"Lucy!" Angela said, "The aunties want to give you a special saint's medal. It is your namesake, Santa Lucia, to remind you of Italy and to bring you back here safely one day."

The old lady in the middle of the trio, stepped forward with a tiny push from her sisters and clasped a silver chain around Lucy's neck. Lucy could see the medal gleaming but she could not make out the figure on its face." She turned to the aunties and said shyly, "*Grazie, grazie!*"

The trio smiled and launched into another speech which Maria reported to be the story of Saint Lucy who delivered gifts to good children on Epiphany Eve. Santa Lucia was known for this task only in Verona, but elsewhere she was revered as the protectress of sight.

Lucy was thrilled at the Verona connection and she wanted to thank each of the aunties in person. When she looked at them now she wondered how she could ever have thought they were identical old crones

"What are their names, Mom?' she asked. "I want to thank them personally."

Maria replied by reaching out to each pair of hands in turn. "This is my aunt Sophia, here is aunt Maria-Teresa and now, aunt Francesca." Lucy was stunned to hear these names that had been handed down through her mother to the next generations in Canada. Lucy had never known the connection before. So many questions crowded her mind but there was no time to ask them.

Amid farewell cries of "*Arrivederci!*" the party of five walked down the stone steps to the lane for the last time. Lucy glanced back to imprint on her memory the shuttered windows with the ornate balconies where the last of the red geraniums bloomed profusely. Next time, she promised herself, I will paint the rest of this beautiful building.

There were tears in several eyes and Lucy did not see Maurizio waving from a side street as they lumbered down the steep hill in the heavily-laden taxi cabs.

Like all travel in these post 9/11 times, the trip to Scotland took most of the day. Everyone was exhausted by the time they were met at the train station in Oban by Anna and Fiona.

The required change of airplane in London, England, and the move to the train in Glasgow, had worn out Susan and Jake. Maria and Lucy were in slightly better shape, but after lugging cases from point to point and checking various schedules, they were both glad of the extra pair of hands Angela provided with the wheelchair.

At one juncture, Lucy whispered to her mother, "How come Angela speaks such good English?"

Maria replied that Angela had trained in the United States before returning to Italy.

Lucy realized once again she had been too involved in herself to find out the most basic things about the family around her in Italy. Opportunities had been missed, but she resolved to do better on that score from now on.

Anna and Fiona immediately took charge of luggage and parcels, leaving the passengers to settle into the comfy seats of Fiona's large van. When the rear door slammed down, Anna assured everyone they would be relaxing in comfort at the farmhouse in only a few minutes.

It was as if she deliberately made this announcement early, knowing that by the time the farmhouse lane was visible, all of her passengers, except Lucy, would be fast asleep.

Anna nodded to Lucy to leave the sleepers and exit the van quietly. There was no point in waking them before the luggage was moved inside. Lucy knew which items belonged to which people, so it was easy to extract the luggage for Susan, Jake and Angela and leave the other cases, and Lucy's specially-wrapped package, in the van.

"Hello, Lucy!" whispered Anna. Thanks for the help with this. Go on inside now. You will find a little surprise in the kitchen."

Lucy walked up the path to the front door of the farmhouse. She knew approximately where the door was, although she had never been there before. Her mother's story about Anna's inheritance had often been told, and Lucy had seen the original aerial photograph of the house that had been sent to London by George, the solicitor who had taken care of Helen Dunlop's affairs and who had contacted Anna after his client's death.

The red-painted door opened into a small room where coats and boots were stored. A partly-open door to the side led into a bright washroom and two more doors ahead of Lucy were conveniently labeled, Kitchen and Lounge. Lucy wondered what one did in a lounge, but moved forward, as requested, into the kitchen.

This was a large room with a welcoming fire, burning brightly, on the end wall of the house. In the middle of the kitchen stood a wooden farmhouse table, similar to the one in the villa.

A huge bank of windows jutted out from where a wall at the front of the house must once have been. There were countertops, cupboards and comfy upholstered chairs and a shiny slate floor underfoot. As Lucy looked at this last item, she saw a cat slink out from under the table and approach to sniff at her feet.

"Well, hi there, puss!" she said softly. "You must be the surprise Aunt Anna mentioned."

Lucy bent down slowly and stroked the thick fur on the back of the brown tabby.

They had never had animals at home when she was growing up and although Lucy had always wanted a dog, there was something soothing about this quiet little cat that looked at her with a trusting face.

"I see you've met our lovely Morag."

Lucy looked up to meet the blue eyes of the young woman who had been driving the van. She was smaller than Lucy in height but looked strong and healthy, if her ruddy complexion was anything to go by.

"Anna's gone out to wake up her visitors. Give me a hand

with these cases. They go into the lounge where there's a pull-down sofa bed. I'll take this case upstairs for Angela. You turn on the kettle, Lucy, and we'll get going right away."

Lucy followed these orders as best she could. It felt like being back at school with the teachers directing you. This Fiona person was used to being obeyed, Lucy decided.

She found the white electric kettle on the counter near a window looking out to the back of the house. Nothing could be seen in the dark, but Lucy was pretty sure there was a mountain out there somewhere.

Fiona's footsteps sounded as she came back down the central stairs and entered the kitchen.

"That's good!" she said, and Lucy felt a jolt of pleasure as she received approval from this organized young woman.

"The supper is ready and everything is prepared for Anna's guests. We'll leave them now and get home to the cottage. It's much smaller than this, Lucy, but you'll enjoy being close to the town and the sea. You can have a quick look around and then get to bed, if you want. I have another run to make tonight to fetch a delivery for the wedding at the hotel, but I'll be back before midnight."

Lucy had almost forgotten that she was supposed to be staying with Fiona. Clearly no protests about that arrangement would be possible and it might be fun to see what life was like in a cottage by the sea.

Bending down, Lucy gave a farewell pat to Morag, who was now purring wildly and weaving around Fiona's booted feet.

They passed Maria on the path outside and Lucy managed to tell her mother to leave her cell phone on in case she needed to contact her, before she had to run to catch up with Fiona who was already waiting by the van.

At least I get to sit at the front this time, Lucy thought, but I won't see much of Oban until tomorrow, I guess.

Chapter Sixteen

ucy woke with a start when a door slammed shut somewhere.

She felt panic when her eyes opened and she thought the roof was falling down onto her head but it was only the steep slant of the wall. She remembered that Fiona had warned her not to sit up quickly or she would get a hard bump.

Rubbing her eyes and yawning widely, Lucy looked around. The air felt cold and she pulled the bedclothes up to her chin, until only her eyes were visible.

Daylight came in through a small window set into the slanted part of the roof above her head. The bedroom was tiny. The single bed and a mini-sized washbasin in one corner was all it contained. Hooks on the wall held Lucy's coat and the clothes she had travelled in. Her suitcase and carry-on bag were under the clothes, against the wall and partly blocked the exit to the door.

Lucy had only a partial memory of the downstairs layout, since Fiona had taken her through to a small kitchen under the stairs and shown her a tray with tea, coffee and sandwiches before leaving on her final driving job of the night. A quick bite to eat and Lucy carried the mug of tea upstairs. She had succumbed to sleep before the mug was empty.

Thinking she had better make an appearance, Lucy had a brief splash in the basin, rubbed her toothbrush over her teeth and dragged her warmest clothes out of her suitcase. She found the wedding outfit in its zipped bag on top of the case and hung it up on one of the hooks thinking her mother would be annoyed if she knew how careless she had been with it.

A comb for her hair was always available in a pocket so that didn't take much time. She dodged around the luggage on the floor and managed to slip out of the door but not without a loud screech from the hinge that must have wakened up anyone who was within hearing.

Lucy took a glance around and saw a couple more doors, one of which must be the freezing washroom she had visited last night, but the hallway was tiny again and she was only a step or two from the stairs. These creaked too, she discovered, but perhaps it wasn't so strange when the whole cottage seemed ancient with huge flowered wallpaper, faded in places, on all the walls.

Descending the steep stairs carefully, as there was no handrail, Lucy found herself facing what must be the cottage's entrance door. To her right was a room with a fireplace, a two-seater couch, an easy chair and a side table. She hardly remembered any of this as there had been no light on when she and Fiona had arrived last night. It was not difficult to find the kitchen again, however, as that was the only other room on the ground floor.

Fiona was not around, unless she was still in bed. Lucy thought she had never seen such a small living space. It was more like a doll's house than anything, although if Fiona lived here alone, it probably was enough for her. Lucy back-tracked to the fireplace where she had glimpsed a set of framed photographs. Since no one was here, she might as well indulge her curiosity.

It took some searching to find Fiona in the pictures but a much younger Fiona was there with a man and woman who were, presumably, her parents. The other pictures showed an older woman with snowy white hair, and a proud smile, whose wrinkled hands were clasped around a pie plate.

Lucy vaguely remembered a story about a 'granny' who cooked and baked for Anna when she first arrived at the farmhouse. This must be Fiona's grandmother.

No one appeared from upstairs. Lucy wandered back to the kitchen, wondering if she should call out to Fiona, then she saw a note on the table.

Help yourself to breakfast, Lucy.
I have to do the Friday school run but
I'll be back after that for an hour or so.
I work in the vet's surgery this afternoon.
Take a look around the town.
I'll find you if you are needed.
Fiona.
PS I left a key on the window ledge.
Lock the door when you leave.

Lucy had to read this note twice to get the significance. Fiona was working again this morning, but it wasn't clear what a 'school run' involved. Obviously she had another job to do in the afternoon. By Lucy's calculations that made three different jobs. Were all Scottish women so busy, she wondered, or is Fiona an exception?

Toast was the simplest meal Lucy could tackle. She found a small bottle of orange juice in the fridge but hesitated to drink it as there would be none left for Fiona. Finding the fridge was a challenge in itself. At first she thought it was a microwave, as it sat on the counter under the only three shelves that were all the storage space available for dishes and cups. As there was no sign of milk anywhere, Lucy finally tried to open the 'microwave' and found the missing fridge.

Bread was in a bin with a rolled top, and butter sat beside it on a china saucer. Lucy was not surprised to find the butter was hard. In Canada it would have been quite soft if left outside the fridge, but here the air was so much cooler and no heating was apparent.

The toaster was coloured bright blue but at least it seemed to work the same way as others Lucy had used. By the time she had figured out how to boil water in the kettle, which sat on an electric stove ring, she was hungry enough to eat and drink anything.

"Well!" she said to the window overlooking a small green area at the back of the cottage.

"I have managed so far. I might as well go out and explore."

She was wearing her hooded sweatsuit but thought it would be wise to run upstairs and fetch her outdoor coat. She took the chance to peek inside the two doors on the landing and found another small bedroom and the bathroom with the smallest bath she had ever seen. Lucy laughed out loud to think how she would have to scrunch herself up to sit in that bath. A vision came to her of the big, luxurious washroom at home in Canada with the separate shower and double sinks. She was beginning to understand that Canadian plumbing standards were not shared by other parts of the world.

Lucy opened the front door of the cottage and was immediately glad that she had turned around to lock the door again. A car had almost touched her as it raced past.

In shock from the close call, Lucy realized there was no sidewalk separating her from the road. The door to the cottage opened right onto the roadway with only the tiniest space between them delineated by a plant pot holding purple pansies.

"Lucky I didn't knock the plant over!" she complained. "I had better watch my step around here."

Fiona's cottage was one of a row of cottages joined together. Observation soon proved to Lucy that the road was for one-way traffic only. By waiting for a space between cars, Lucy was able to sprint across the road and reach a paved pathway bordering an area of bushes and small trees. A cold wind was blowing through this barrier and she clutched the hood of her coat closer to her as she followed the path away from Fiona's cottage.

In a few moments she came to the end of the barrier and was almost swept off her feet by the force of the wind. She caught her breath but it was not the cold air that had startled her.

She was looking out to sea and an amazing scene opened up in front of her.

The waves were pounding on a small sandy beach almost at her feet. Further out she could see a little boat rocking in the waves as it headed for land, and beyond the boat an island took up the middle distance. Clouds scurried across the sky but Lucy could glimpse a larger island farther away.

This was like nothing Lucy had ever seen before. Car trips to the Great Lakes near London, did not reveal scenes like this. Lakes were serene and controlled even in the winter when ice filled the shoreline. It was rare to see anything on the horizon and certainly not islands.

She felt she could have watched the little boat struggle against the wind and waves for hours but the cold was beginning to penetrate her clothing and rather than turn back to the cottage, Lucy decided to venture onto the beach and, hopefully, shelter from the worst of the wind.

This was accomplished by first walking carefully through a patch of tall, sharp-pointed grass. A large rock near the shoreline provided a handy place to lean against and, as she had suspected, the wind gusted by above her head.

"Well, this is different!" she said. "I didn't expect to find myself on a beach in November!

The weather and the scenery are such a contrast to the

villa in Italy. I'll stay here and warm up a bit then look further along that road and see what I can find."

Lucy watched seagulls following the boat and figured out it must have a catch of fish on board.

When the boat had gone from her view she took off a glove and dabbled in the sand with her fingers, soon uncovering tiny pink shells which she slipped into her coat pocket.

With her gaze on the sea again, she was startled to see a dark head pop up several metres away. She watched intently, hardly believing what she saw. It happened again and this time she could make out the gleam of eyes. Could this be a seal? Obviously the sea around Scotland was a lot different from anything Lucy had experienced before.

With her attention on the seals, Lucy failed to notice that waves had crept up towards her new leather boots. Just in time, she felt dampness in the sand and leaped up to find the tide was rising with each small wave.

"I will have a lot to ask Fiona about," she concluded. "That's if I ever meet up with her again!"

After dusting off the sand from the back of her coat, Lucy marched swiftly along the road and around a corner past a grove of trees, and found herself in the middle of a busy town.

She calculated that this must be Oban and set off to explore. There were small shops on both sides of the main street but this street also was for one-way traffic. It took some time to understand the system as cars were parked on both sides, facing in all directions.

"I think I'll stick to this side for now," she decided. "Crossing the road looks to be hazardous!"

She looked in store windows, finding nothing of great interest, but she nodded at people who passed her. Everyone smiled, so she got the impression the natives, at least, were friendly.

A delicious smell of bacon wafted towards her from a storefront where two tables indicated a restaurant serving breakfast. Lucy suddenly felt pangs of hunger. She really hadn't had a decent meal for a whole day. Searching in her pockets she found a ten dollar bill. That should be enough for coffee and bacon and eggs, she decided. Her hand was on the door handle and she was just about to pull, when it struck her that they might not want dollars in Scotland. She stopped and considered what she could do.

Her mother was too far away to help. A bank would not want to exchange such a small amount of money, even if she found one nearby. The longer she spent by the door looking at the happy eaters inside, the stronger her hunger became. She was just about to stomp away in frustration when a hand on her shoulder stopped her.

"There you are! I was wondering where you got to. Good idea this. Let's go inside."

Before she could say a word, Fiona had opened the door, ushered Lucy inside and found a vacant table, all the while exchanging conversation with seated customers in a gibberish language that was completely unintelligible to her companion.

Lucy had not yet said one word to Fiona. She was quite intimidated by this forceful person who seemed so comfort-able in a place where Lucy definitely did not fit in.

"So what have you been up to this morning?" began Fiona, removing her gloves and shrugging off her coat. The heat inside the restaurant began to overwhelm Lucy. She could feel her face flush red so she hurried to divest herself of a layer or two just as the coffee arrived in small cups but accompanied with a pair of metal jugs holding what Lucy hoped was second servings.

"I've been looking around some," she replied, "but can I ask you what you were saying before? I couldn't understand a word."

"Ah, many people in this part of Scotland speak the Gaelic. It's the old language of the country."

"I see. And what does a 'school run' mean and how do

you manage so many different jobs and did I really see a seal in the sea today and how often does the tide come in or out and how do I pay for food with only Canadian dollars?" It all came out in a rush and Lucy felt like a small child for blurting everything out at once.

Fiona just laughed and replied patiently, "I pick up and deliver children who live far from the primary school in town here. That takes an hour or so every morning and afternoon on week days. I also run a taxi service for adults who need help getting to shopping or doctor appointments and, with my partner, who shares the costs of the van, we do overnight deliveries to hotels and stores."

"But you said you worked at the vet's as well." Lucy was confused trying to fit all this activity into one person's 24 hours.

"Yes, that's a part-time job once or twice a week. I am really a college student in Inverness most of the time but when there are holidays, or I am working on location assignments for my courses, I pick up my usual work here."

Lucy could not believe Fiona's busy lifestyle. "How do you manage all this and what are you studying to be?"

"It's all a matter of planning. You can do a lot if you are organized and I learned it fast when my parents died and it was just Granny and me."

Lucy was beginning to realize how lucky her privileged, easy life in Canada was, compared to this whirlwind of a woman who was not much older than Lucy herself.

"I am going to be a wildlife conservation officer when I qualify and, yes, you probably did see a seal. The sea is alive with them around these parts. As for the tides; they come in and out twice daily. There are tables published to tell you when to expect them in each season."

Lucy was grateful she did not have to comment further on Fiona's life as plates of steaming food had arrived at their table. Fiona must have ordered for Lucy, another example of her 'take charge' style, but she was not about to complain when the aroma of the food hit her nostrils.

The next five minutes were occupied with consuming bacon, eggs and sausages, tomato, mushrooms and fried bread. Lucy had never eaten so much for breakfast in her life but she cleared the plate and wiped her mouth reaching for more coffee.

"That was delicious, Fiona, but, as I said before, I have no Scottish money with me."

"Oh, never fear! Anna gave me twenty pounds for you. I'll pay for your meal from that. There should be plenty left for anything small you might want."

"That was kind of Aunt Anna," said Lucy, with relief.

"Kind does not begin to describe that lady's character," began Fiona, in a more serious tone of voice than Lucy had heard from her so far. "She has made an enormous difference in my life, I can tell you. I wouldn't be taking this college course if she hadn't coached me through my English exams and she has treated me like a daughter in every way. You are lucky to have an aunt like Anna, believe me!"

Lucy swallowed quickly and replied, "She's not a real aunt. My mother's friends have always been honorary aunts to me and my sister. It's just a habit to call them that but I suppose I am too old now to continue."

"I'd say you were lucky to have someone like Anna in your life in any capacity at all. She has done a lot for this community as well. She's a remarkable lady!"

Lucy's previous opinion of Anna was undergoing a re-think as Fiona spoke. Privately, she thought Fiona was going to get a surprise when she got to know Susan, the acknowledged leader of the Sambas, and also her own mother, Maria, who was a diva in the London, Ontario, fashion world.

Fiona put down her cup and spread orange marmalade on her third slice of toast as she asked, "So what do you do, Lucy? I hear you have had a fine holiday in Italy."

Lucy felt she was put on the spot. She could not compare

with Fiona's busy life, but she had to say something. "Yes, we had a good time at the villa where my mother's mother was born. Actually, I painted some pictures there for my grand-mother in Toronto."

"That's interesting! I do wildlife photography myself. In fact a couple of my pictures are in here."

Lucy turned to where Fiona pointed and saw the pictures of foxes and hawks with discreet cards fixed to the frames announcing the prices.

"I sell the odd one here," continued Fiona, "but my best customer is the vet who hangs them on his surgery walls. Have you ever considered selling your work, Lucy?"

"Oh, I am still at college studying arts and design." She thought this sounded lame so she rushed on. "I am into clothes design for teens at the moment and I am planning to display my ideas in a section of my mother's store soon."

Lucy was shocked to hear this declaration come out of her mouth. In truth, there was no such plan but she suddenly realized that it was something she really wanted and she determined in that moment to work hard to make it happen.

"Good for you!" commented Fiona. "You are never too young to get a foot in the door."

She rose from her seat with a purposeful air, grabbed her padded car coat and delivered her next orders while simulta-neously depositing cash onto the table and handing the remaining pound notes to Lucy.

"Can you amuse yourself for an hour or so? I'll be back to take you to the hotel. We have place name cards for tables and drink orders to deliver to the kitchens.

Everyone will assemble at Anna's this evening for dinner. You'll meet Alan and Kirsty there."

Before Lucy could ask where she would meet Fiona, that lady was out the door, waving to friends at other tables, and walking briskly away.

Chapter Seventeen

❧

Mom whr r u? im stuck here iv climbd a hill & walkd all ovr obn
Nvr cn enythng lik ths b4.
U wd LOL 2 c Fionas hows SOOO tiny but shes very bizy &
keepin me wrkng this aft. C u ltr?
Lu

Maria found this text message on her phone and struggled to decipher it. It seemed like Lucy was all right for now and Fiona was in charge. She confirmed this with Jeanette, who was more familiar with teen text speak.

Jeanette laughed at the message. "She couldn't be in better hands, Maria! Fiona is a powerhouse and does more in one day than most young folks manage in a week."

Maria was content with this. She would call her daughter soon. She turned back to the conversation she was having with Jeanette about style in fashion and furnishings.

The two women had become friends immediately on Maria's arrival at George and Jeanette's home the previous evening. Maria thought it was the Canadian connection that made the instant bond, but it could have been the way she warmed to Liam, their gorgeous little boy who had his father's curly fair hair and hazel eyes a shade lighter than his mother's.

This morning's conversation had moved on to the urgent topic of wedding apparel. Jeanette had been busy with Liam and design work she was doing for Bev and Alan's home. Shopping for clothes had taken a back seat and now she was desperate.

Once Liam was down for his nap, Maria happily took charge and reviewed everything Jeanette had hanging in her wardrobe.

"I don't need anything fancy here in Oban," apologized Jeanette. "It's all about washable stuff and the odd skirt and jacket for business. I had very little warning about this event and I can't see what's suitable in this lot."

"I will be wearing a business suit myself, Jeanette," offered Maria. "I would feel happier if you were in the same sort of outfit. Let's see what we can do."

Maria shuffled through the hangers in a professional manner and Jeanette just stood back and let the expert do her work. If Maria could salvage appropriate dress from this motley collection, she was prepared to applaud heartily.

"I see the problem," Maria muttered. "There's not much that matches but you do have some good quality items here."

"Those would be my pre-pregnancy clothes from Canada," Jeanette conceded ruefully. "I'm not too sure they all fit me nowadays."

"Well, let's see what the possibilities are!" asserted Maria in a confident manner.

Within five minutes she had selected a long navy jacket and a purple flared skirt and instructed Jeanette to try these on. Jeanette emerged from the bathroom with a disgruntled expression on her face. "I don't think these go together, Maria, and the skirt won't button properly at the waist."

Maria looked her subject up and down with a practiced eye and declared that the jacket just needed a good belt, the skirt was a nice length and when a scarf had been added the colours would blend perfectly.

Jeanette still felt apprehensive. "I'm not sure about this and what do I do about the waistline?"

"Well, preferably we could get an alteration done, but there's no time for that. I know an old, temporary trick that will work if you have any elastic on hand."

Jeanette nodded and found a length of white elastic in her sewing basket. Maria asked for needle and thread and quickly sewed a loop of elastic to circle the skirt's button and attached it to the buttonhole, giving Jeanette two inches of extra room at the waist.

Once the outfit was assembled again, Maria picked a slim purple belt for the jacket and assured Jeanette she had the perfect scarf in her own luggage that would complement the colours and tie the outfit together.

Black court shoes and a short-sleeved top, long enough to conceal the waistband, completed the transformation.

"I never would have thought of this combination, Maria! You would think it would be obvious to me when arranging colours and patterns for furnishings is my business. It's much harder when it's yourself you are decorating."

"It's what I do all the time," explained Maria, "but I doubt I could have assembled the antique furniture and fabrics you picked for Anna's lounge. The effect is so comfortable and yet so stylish. Susan and Jake will love staying there."

This comment redirected the conversation to the topic of the dinner party to be held at Anna's farmhouse in the evening.

"It's usually a formal occasion when a dinner is held the night before the wedding," advised Jeanette, "but Anna assured me it would be very casual under the circumstances. It's a chance for everyone to get together and congratulate the happy couple."

"I will be delighted to do that. It is wonderful of Bev and Anna to arrange for us to be here for such a special event.

Susan and I are so happy for Bev and anxious to meet Alan for the first time."

"Oh, you'll love Alan! He's the very best kind of Scotsman, tall and rugged and single-focused. At the moment his focus is on Bev and she's in seventh heaven."

Maria laughed at this description. "I hope you are not casting aspersions on your own lovely Scotsman, Jeanette? He's the one who made all this happen for Anna and I think he's quite dashing, from the short time I've met him."

"Funny you should say that, Maria. You had better be prepared to do some dancing tomorrow night with my husband. He's a demon at the *Dashing* White Sergeant, one of the popular dances around these parts."

"Thanks for the warning, Jeanette. I'd better take some alternative footwear with me. These heels are not meant for dancing."

❦

As dusk descended over the hills, the party assembled at Anna's farmhouse. Susan, Jake and Angela greeted Maria, Lucy and Fiona and waited in the lounge while Fiona fetched Kirsty and the bride and groom from the nearby farm. Jeanette, George and Liam were the last to arrive and by then the party was in full swing.

"You'd think this lot hadn't seen each other in ages," suggested Fiona to Anna when she saw the way everyone welcomed each new arrival.

"Well, it's not so much that they have been apart for so long," explained Anna, as the two assembled the hors d'oevres that had been delivered from Fiona's van on her last trip.

"It's more that so much has happened in a short time to everyone. Jake and Susan have been through a traumatic experience and Lucy and Maria have accomplished a great mother daughter blending as you can see from their attitude to each other. Bev and Eric have been here with Alan and Kirsty for some months and the decisions they have made are only now coming to fruition. It's the *amount* of change they have all dealt with that causes them to feel the long separation is over. And remember that not everyone here knows everyone else. There are new bonds to be formed, as happens whenever there is a marriage."

Fiona watched and listened as Kirsty told how keen she was to 'get these two married' so she could retire to Skye and an easy life at last. When pressed, she said she would miss Eric the most but he should visit her often and continue their exchange of stories from two sides of the Atlantic. Eric smiled at this invitation. He knew Alan had bought a computer for his mother so all of them could keep in touch through Skype.

Fiona had to agree that it was a happy reunion for everyone. The farmhouse was overflowing with warmth and laughter but Fiona knew the reunions were not over for the night.

Anna's brother Philip was due to arrive in an hour or so with a special passenger. He was driving from Manchester to surprise Anna and to meet her Canadian friends about whom he had heard so much. Philip's long journey from Egypt had been kept secret from all except Jay. They had met up in Manchester after Philip had a night's rest there.

Fiona hugged this little kernel of knowledge to herself and pictured Anna's face when Philip arrived at the door with Bev's son James.

Meanwhile, there was a roast beef meal to serve and champagne to pour. Fiona knew it would be a busy, joyful evening and another late night for her. Kirsty, in superstitious mode, had insisted that Bev would go to the hotel overnight so the groom would not see his bride before the ceremony. Bev could drive there later with Philip and James. That left only Lucy to be returned to Fiona's cottage.

With Lucy's help, she had checked that everything at the grand old Highland Hotel on the hillside was ready for the wedding, so she planned an easy morning for both of them before her chauffeuring duties would begin again. She thought with some pleasure of the bright red skirt and ruffled white blouse Anna had insisted on buying for her, along with a brown fur-collared leather coat that made her feel like a million dollars, as they said in Canada.

Bev held tight to her elder son all the way from Anna's to the hotel in town. They had been separated for months while James completed his business studies in England and she could not believe how mature he now seemed. There was a hint of an English accent there too, although James was quick to accuse his mother of a Scottish lilt infiltrating her familiar Canadian speech.

"How did your term exams go, James?"

"Well, I don't have the results yet but I feel pretty confident. I was able to use my work with A Plus as a case study and I had all the details on my laptop, so that was easy."

"Have you heard from that nice girl Caroline?"

"Now don't go fishing for information, Mom! We are just friends but we text once in a while.

She's at the London School of Economics. She says she might do Social Services work when she qualifies but I think she's a born politician."

"Really! That's interesting! I would think that line of work demands many years of apprenticing to political parties."

"I suppose so. Remember the project she did in college with her great-gran's nursing home?

The way she rallied the forces to accomplish that work says to me she is able to influence people and that is the foundation of political life, I think."

Philip interjected from the driver's seat as conversation from his passengers lapsed for a moment. "I'd say you have persuasive talents yourself, young man, if our talks on the way here from Manchester are anything to go by."

"What do you mean, Philip?" enquired Bev.

"Just that James has talked Anna and Alina into a new venture for their company. Isn't it called something like New Again?"

"The final decision on the name was Renew Again." James turned to his mother to explain.

"You know how people find a sweater or even a knitted dress or something that fits perfectly and you wear it so often that the thing eventually falls apart?"

As James spoke, Bev remembered a story of Maria's about a replacement sweater she had once found for Anna's husband, to win a bet. "I know what you mean, James! I have a few old things I'm clinging on to in the hopes of finding another of the same type, but that never happens."

"Yes! That's it! So the idea I had was that customers could send in photos and measurements of the original garments and the A Plus knitters could make a brand new version of it for them. It's been very popular already and Alina's heading up the new department from Canada."

"That's an excellent idea, James. Well done!"

The mention of Alina's name reminded Bev of a quiet moment she had shared with Anna shortly after her arrival at the farmhouse. She had asked why Alina had not come with Anna as their plan was that all the Sambas would be able to attend her wedding.

Anna had tearfully confessed the secret about Alina's fading eyesight and now Bev wondered what the repercussions of this development would mean to the company the two women had worked so hard to establish.

They had reached Oban now and the car engine was changing gear as it climbed the winding road up towards McCaig's Folly, passing fine Victorian mansions, some of which had signs declaring their B&B services.

Bev watched for the smaller house with the spectacular

view over the bay, that Jeanette and George had bought, and noticed new paint on the front porch.

The party was welcomed into the hotel and soon shown to their respective rooms for the night. James carried his mother's wedding gown in a clothing bag and also her overnight case and the honeymoon luggage. As he set these down in the room and examined an enormous vase of fragrant stargazer lilies contributed by the hotel staff, Bev asked him to stay for a minute.

"I didn't want to ask you this in the car, James, it's too personal." James settled down on the side of the double bed and waited for his mother's question.

"Are you happy with my decision to marry Alan?"

"You know I think he's a great guy, Mom. Why are you asking now?"

"It's just that you have more memories of your father than Eric does and I need to be sure you feel I haven't jumped too fast into this relationship, with all the changes it means for all of us."

"It seems to me that changes come anyway, Mom. I had already moved to the UK for much of my time and Eric loves it here. He has really claimed Kirsty as a grandmother and he's doing well at school, or so he tells me."

Bev paused. James was not answering the main question about Alan and she began to be apprehensive.

James could read his mother's face as easily as she could read his.

"Look, Mom! I am *very* pleased for you. I have never seen you so happy and if Alan Matthews is the cause of that, I could never complain about it."

Bev knew her elder son well and was not satisfied with this explanation.

"What is it you're not telling me James?"

"Really, it's nothing major. I wonder sometimes what it is you are taking on with the farm animals and Alan's life outside in all weathers. It's so different from all you have known before and, honestly, I want an easier life for you after the years you spent devoted to Eric and me. You deserve an easier life now. That's all it is and I didn't mean to say any of this at all."

James jumped up and caught his mother in an embrace to hide the emotions he was feeling at this disclosure. The last thing he wanted was to cast any blight on this special occasion for his mother. Over her shoulder he proclaimed, "Now don't worry! None of this will come out in my speech tomorrow, Mom. It's all good, believe me!"

Bev was too choked up to answer. She patted James' shoulders instead. She knew she had been blessed with two wonderful sons but, at this moment, she understood how much like his strong, responsible and caring father, James had become.

Gathering herself together with some difficulty, Bev stated, "Don't worry about me, James. Alan and I have plans for the future. Now off you go to bed, my dear one, or you will not be fit to steer me down the aisle tomorrow. Sleep well, James. I love you."

James made a quick exit before he embarrassed himself with tears. As he made his way down the hall he made a vow to hold back his emotions at the ceremony. This was clearly going to be difficult for him to do, but he resolved to represent his family in the best possible way, no matter what it might cost him.

Chapter Eighteen

Saturday morning displayed a cloud-streaked blue sky. Fiona, who had been up early enough to see the dawn, informed Lucy that the weather would clear by the afternoon and the wedding at five o'clock would take place in the last rays of the sunset. With this confident assertion, she reached for the teapot and poured herself another large mug of tea.

Lucy was surprised to note that Fiona had come downstairs to the kitchen wearing a thick brown robe tied around her middle that looked as much like a bearskin as Lucy had ever seen. This casual wear made Fiona seem much more approachable, so Lucy settled back in her chair and prepared to get answers to a number of questions she had been storing up. Everyone was so busy talking to each other last night at Anna's place that she had no time to ask trivial questions.

"So you are not working this morning, Fiona?" she began.

"Well, no school run of course, but I do have to spend an hour or two with the vet later."

"Good! I wanted to ask you about the cat I saw. She disappeared during dinner but I wondered if she had anything to do with the wildcat I had heard stories about."

Fiona laughed. "You mean Sylvester! If you had seen him

you would know the difference in a second. Anna and I visited him in his new home a couple of months ago and he is huge. The keepers say he is even bigger than the usual Scottish wild cat and they put it down to the exceptional care he received as a kitten. He still knows our voices and comes up to us, purring madly."

"That was quite some story about his mother being killed and you taking over. I'm sorry I missed seeing him. So Morag is a new cat?"

"Sure now! Kirsty found her in her barn, trying to get milk from the cows. She ignored her for a while but the wee thing was always around so she knew she had been abandoned. Farm country folk are not always sympathetic to stray animals but Morag was a sweet wee one. Anna wanted her because she had a bit of Sylvester's colouring, and I look after her when Anna is in Canada."

"That's kind of you. I always wanted a pet, myself, but my parents were too busy to take on the responsibility."

"I imagine you could look after an animal by yourself, Lucy," suggested Fiona with some surprise. "If you want something bad enough there's always a way to make it happen."

She stopped to sip her tea and added, "By the way, I asked your Mum to let me see your paintings last night. They had been left in the back of the van the other night and I thought they might be safer indoors. She said I could take a peek."

Lucy was astounded that her mother had agreed to this without mentioning it to her but curiosity about Fiona's opinion soon overtook her annoyance. "What did you think about them?"

"I thought they were remarkably well done. You should do more work and develop your own style, Lucy. Your mother is very proud of you, you know. I hope you understand how lucky you are."

Before Lucy could summon a response to this, Fiona stood, rinsed her cup in the sink and announced she was heading for a bath. "There should be enough hot water for the both of us. I won't fill the bath just in case we run out."

Lucy was left alone to think about Fiona's comments. This young woman, living an independent and productive life had good advice to give. Lucy was beginning to think someone had intended to put the two of them together and she was beginning to understand why.

৩৯৪৩

Kirsty was looking out of her bedroom window and thinking that this view that had been familiar to her through the seasons for fifty years would, after today, be supplanted by a far different view from the windows of her room in Skye. After the wedding celebrations she would leave with family members to settle into her new home. She was looking forward to the sights and smells of the sea that she had loved as a child, but she was also leaving behind a lifetime of memories in this place.

There was her life with her dear husband, Malcolm, and their early days establishing a viable farm with baby Alan slung on the back of either one of them. It was no wonder Alan had taken to the farm work when he had absorbed the smells and sounds from such an early age.

Those were hard but happy times and the memories made her smile.

She preferred to forget the shock of finding her husband lying in the cowshed, dead from a massive stroke, and the time it had taken her to get back into life again. 'Life is for the living', they always said, and the years after Malcolm's death had been satisfying, with Alan to look after and the animals to care for.

The only regret she had had about getting old was that Alan would be left alone one day. The thought of him at the farm on his own was one that had worried her in the midnight hours.

His life on the hills in all weathers had always made contact with women difficult, but now, fate had brought him a wife in such an unexpected way.

Kirsty sighed happily as she thought of Bev. Such a fine woman with two lovely boys who were a credit to her style of mothering, and Bev was a good friend of Anna's to boot. Kirsty's connection to Anna had deepened from the first moment they met during the swine flu crisis, and whenever Anna or her friend Alina were in Scotland, they made sure to visit with Kirsty.

It was an invitation to tea at Anna's estate house that had first introduced Kirsty and Alan to Bev and Eric.

Kirsty was so glad to have Eric in her life now. The grand-child she had never thought to have, was an important part of her thoughts for the future. There was much she wanted to pass on to him and, (thanks be to God!), the boy was not only interested in her old stories but he had settled down in Oban and seemed to be thriving at high school. His expertise with the modern phones and computers and that internet thingy, as she called it, had made him instantly popular with teachers and students.

And today, it was all coming together as new lives began for all of them. Kirsty reached down and closed the window. It would be a fine November day for the wedding. Crisp and cold, for sure, but bright, to welcome the family from Skye and the Canadians who were now family also.

She was pleased the Canadians would see Oban in all its splendour from the hotel's viewpoint, and delighted that they would experience a traditional ceilidh that she knew would tell them more about Alan and his people than any amount of talking and explaining could ever do.

A great day to look forward to, she decided, and turned with a happy sigh to make her preparations.

꧁꧂

From noon onwards, the Highland Hotel had been humming with activity. Manageress, Catriona McTavish, a distant relative of Kirsty's family, already knew she would be overrun with the Skye folk who had arrived in local B&Bs or were staying with other nearby family.

The fact they were not in the hotel itself was no barrier to their constant interruptions, disguised as polite inquiries as to "whether they could help out a wee bittie with anything at all, at all?"

Catriona had assigned the younger members to helping the florist set out the arrangements of carnations and ferns in the ballroom where the ceremony was to be held. She insisted on keeping control over the seating in the centre area and the decoration of the bridal arch where the couple would take their vows. The caterer would supervise the round tables for eight where the meal would be served and an experienced crew of hotel staff would whip away the guest chairs after the ceremony and replace them at the tables. This would leave a substantial area cleared for the essentials: the band, the bar and the dancing.

Catriona had checked on progress in the kitchens and all was well there in the capable hands of John, the head chef. She still had worries, however, regarding the unknown number of people who might descend on the hotel for the event. Skye folk had been arriving by ferry for two days now and she was afraid they would overwhelm the entire enterprise. She had had a quiet word with John about this and extra supplies were on hand in the kitchen to meet whatever eventualities should occur.

She checked her watch for the umpteenth time. The bride was safely in her room and Jeanette was bringing one of the Canadian women to help her dress. The bride's son, a late arrival, had been seen watching proceedings and taking photographs from the front entrance, but he was no trouble. She saw him rubbing his hands in front of the blazing fire, opposite her desk in the reception hall. A tall, good-looking lad, she thought. There should be some fine photographs.

She had set aside a room on this level for family pictures after the ceremony, while the ballroom was being prepared. At this thought, she turned and rushed to the room to make sure the florist had followed her directions and set up a stand with flowers as a background to the photographs.

In some ways she would be glad when this day was over, although she was certain it would be well into Sunday before the hotel settled down. Thankfully there were few other guests here this weekend as the noise would definitely cause complaints. Catriona had placed these guests on the top floor of the hotel, as far from the celebrations as possible. The views from up there were so spectacular they hardly noticed the extra stairs.

If all went as planned, she hoped she might even get to kick up her heels for a time. It was sure to be a great night.

☙❧

The Canadian contingent were to talk about the wedding for years afterward.

Not one of them had ever experienced anything like it. From the moment the stirring sound of the pipes began and Bev was led down the hotel stairs on the arm of a very proud James, with Liam bobbing down to the altar before them, scattering white heather from a basket; all the way to the last, ferocious Strip-the-Willow dance, the entire event was exceptional in every way.

Not only was Bev absolutely glowing in the beautiful dress Alina had created for her, but Alan, also, was a sight to behold in his tartan kilt and black evening jacket with antique silver buttons and a froth of lace at cuffs and neck. It was hard to recognize him at first as the quiet, casually-dressed man they had met the night before at Anna's. Lucy whispered to her mother about the dagger tucked into Alan's knee socks and was hushed by Anna who said it was a *skean dhu* and required to defend his wife-to-be from danger of enemy attack. As Lucy looked around the crowded ballroom full of hefty Highland men in tartan kilts and sporrans, she figured there was no danger of that tonight.

The bride and groom made a handsome couple but what caused eyes to tear up, was not their appearance so much as the look of absolute certainty they exchanged at the simple altar when they said their vows. At this juncture, Fiona passed along the row, spotless, lace-edged handkerchiefs of her granny's she had brought with her for just this eventuality, and all the women discreetly dabbed at their eyes, to Eric's dismay.

As Bev and Alan had wished, the ceremony was simple and short and soon the couple were parading down the central aisle again, hand in hand and with matching smiles, as the guests stood, cheering and clapping madly.

Photographs followed to mark the occasion and in the small room, a refreshing glass of champagne was raised in the first toast. Alan saluted Bev's friends who had travelled far to support her this day. He said he would never forget them and hoped they would not be strangers in the future. With one accord, all the Canadians assured Alan they would be back whenever they could.

Another ceremonial entrance followed, as the piper led them into the ballroom again for the wedding supper. Anna and Fiona were seated with a group of Kirsty's relatives and Maria, Susan and Jake joined a table where local people warmly welcomed them as Anna's friends.

James, Eric and Lucy were spirited away to a table where younger guests from Skye were assembled and they enjoyed the banter across the table after the Canadians had deciphered the accents enough to understand what was being said to them. Lucy was able to inform the other two that the odd burst of strange language was Gaelic but Eric surprised them by adding a toast in the language, which he had begun to learn at school.

The bride and her new husband sat with Kirsty and the senior members of her family from Skye at a table only slightly ahead of, and facing the rest of the guests. Both of them had requested the minimum number of speeches and so with James' salute to the couple and a humorous anecdote or two from Alan's cousin, the room was soon cleared to set up for the dancing.

The guests gathered in the reception area and enjoyed the scent of the peat fire while they got to know one another better. Lucy was assured she would have partners for the Scottish country dances who would lead her through the moves. She noticed a bottle of whisky being passed around and wondered if the partners would be fit to show her how to do the steps.

Mr. and Mrs. Matthews retired to their room upstairs and appeared after a few minutes in a change of clothing. Bev was now wearing a white full-length dress with a broad tartan sash across it which matched Alan's mother's tartan. He had removed his jacket and dress shirt and was wearing a plain white shirt with sleeves rolled up to show his muscular forearms.

The newly-married couple proudly led the way back into the ballroom where the lights were dimmed and a band of fiddlers, a harpist, a drummer and a pianist were already set up and playing merrily. A tall man in tartan trousers and waistcoat stood behind a microphone and invited everyone to take their partners for The Gay Gordons.

Maria rushed to her daughter's side and handed her a pair of the new foldable ballet slippers she had carried in her purse. "Quick, put these on! I'll take your high heels. Anna says these dances are wild!"

Lucy had no sooner made the switch than the music started and she was swept along with a cousin of Alan's who introduced himself as Seamus Dhu, owing to his black hair, he said.

The dance was for couples and consisted of a march around the room with hands held above the shoulders for about eight beats. Lucy was just getting accustomed to this part when with a quick switch of arms, she was marching in the opposite direction around the circle and then twirled dizzily under Seamus' outstretched arm for several more beats, ending up in both his arms for a mad, turning gallop to complete the sequence. Hoping that was all she was required to do, Lucy breathed deeply and set off again with Seamus' expert guidance. Conversation was impossible owing to the whoops and cheers that resounded through the room and almost drowned out the music. She soon discovered it was all about the beat. The drum could be felt through the floor boards and as long as she listened to that rhythm she could keep up with the rest of the dancers.

A Dashing White Sergeant dance followed and this was designed to allow Lucy to meet all the other dancers. She stayed in position in the middle of two young men and progressed around the hall ducking under the arms of trios with two females and a man in the centre. The whole thing took enormous concentration and it was only when she sat out to catch her breath that she saw the intricate patterns made by the experienced dancers like Fiona and Jeanette with George in the middle. The scene was a blur of colour as the men's kilts and women's skirts flew by. Lucy sipped a cold coke and wondered if she would ever see anything like it again.

A slow dance, accompanied by the harp, gave everyone a chance to recoup their energy and allowed Bev and Alan to lead off together, then split apart to invite Susan and Maria, James and Eric to join them on the dance floor. Soon the floor was full of couples swirling around to the delicate sounds of the harp. Some of the dancers were singing.

The music the harpist played sounded familiar to Maria.

She knew she had heard it before and after a moment she identified it as a waltz version of the old song;

> *"It's now or never, come hold me tight.*
> *Kiss me my darling be mine tonight.*
> *Tomorrow may be too late*
> *It's now or never, my love won't wait!"*

As the words and melody of the chorus ran through her mind, Maria remembered where she had heard the music before. Her father used to play a record of Italian favourites for her mother when Maria was small. An Italian tenor sang the soaring melodies and her mother loved this tune in particular.

"Come dance with me, *Cara Mia*!" her father would beg, and her mother would untie her apron and float into his arms to dance around the kitchen floor as the sentimental old song was played.

Now or never. There's a message there for me, Maria thought. So many things and people we take for granted in life and none of us knows how long we have to appreciate them. She looked over at Susan and Jake chatting with local people and wondered what the future would hold for them.

She suddenly felt a deep pang of longing for Paul. Did he truly understand he was the love of her life? How wonderful it would be if he could be here with her tonight for this amazing occasion. Would they celebrate Lucy's wedding together on some distant day just like they had when Theresa married?

Maria suddenly realized the separation from her husband and daughter had gone on long enough and she could not wait to get back home.

Chapter Nineteen

A ngela had asked to be excused from the wedding celebrations at the hotel in order to make notes on the final days of her therapy treatment for Jake.

When Anna's friends had left on Saturday afternoon with Fiona, Angela was glad of the peace of the old, stone building and she settled down in the kitchen with Morag for company.

She had not had much time to consider the implications of the combined massage and mindful

meditation she had developed for Jake, and it was important for her to get her thoughts down on paper before the experience faded from both her physical, and mental, memory.

The entire process had been experimental, but there was solid research to back up the individual elements. Angela had always believed that massage was most beneficial when applied by someone who, like herself, had what the old folks called "the healing hands".

The meditation aspect was new to her but her reading on the subject indicated that concentration was the key. She would sit with Jake as he worked through the program and she learned with him each day.

Jake was an apt pupil. Angela had found those who had

suffered pain or disability were already able to focus their minds to a degree far greater than the normal, healthy sector of the population.

The hours spent with Jake at the villa were unforgettable now. Her pen raced over the pages as she captured the details of their sessions. At first, Jake was heavily medicated and very tense from the stress of travel and the mental shock he had received at the clinic. It took a few days of hour-long massage and relaxing environmental sounds before he could release the tension in his muscles and begin to benefit. As he voluntarily dropped the medications and was able to respond to the muscle stimulation, his ability to support his weakened frame out of the wheelchair improved greatly. At this point the meditation therapy began. It was based very simply on positive thinking; a way of drawing healing into the mind to match the feelings of comfort engendered by the massage. To Angela's amazement, the two therapies complemented each other in an almost miraculous way.

Of course, Jake was just one example, she cautioned herself, and the results he experienced could not be considered to be typical of all patients or clients. Much more research and practical application needed to be done before definitive statements could be made, but Angela was thrilled with Jake's progress and for now that was sufficient.

She consulted her daily notes for confirmation that Jake's improvement had begun to be evident from the fourth day of the program. Although such intensive time and attention could not be afforded by many MS sufferers, it had been most worthwhile for Angela to donate the time with Jake as he was able to identify for her the specific areas of his body where he felt improvement.

Susan gladly confirmed that her husband's depression had lifted and he seemed more comfortable communicating with her. He could also move more freely.

The effects of the villa itself and its location above the peaceful vineyards and olive groves could not be discounted, but Angela agreed with Susan that vast improvements had been achieved.

Angela also noted that their short time in Scotland had demonstrated that the location was not the guiding factor as Jake had continued to improve and was even willing to try to stay for some of the evening at the wedding.

Angela wondered if she could find a journal that might publish her notes and share her discoveries with a wider audience in the professions.

She was just finishing the detail on the last few days when she heard Fiona's van draw up at the garden gate and the voices of Anna, Susan and Jake could be heard laughing as they wheeled Jake's chair up to the front door.

Angela gently removed a sleeping Morag to another chair seat and closed up her notebook. One final check with her patient and the main portion of her work would be completed.

"Now, what is all this hilarity about?" she asked, with a smile to match the faces that arrived at the door. "Have you been keeping my prize patient up too late?"

Jake replied with a snort of denial. "*I* could have stayed much longer but these two worry-warts insisted it was time to go!" He turned and blew a kiss to each of the ladies to show he was joking with them. Angela noticed how easy that movement was for him and made another mental note to include it.

"Angela!" he exclaimed, "I had a great chat with the local doc here and with the vet too. You won't believe it but both of them are keen on massage for people *and* animals. I told them what we had been doing in Italy and they are immensely interested in the work."

"Now, enough talking, Jake! You don't want to overtire yourself and give Angela a poor impression of your health when she has done so much to help you improve."

Susan wheeled Jake into the small washroom near the

door and left him there to wash up before bed, confident he was now able to manage on his own for a minute or two.

She reached into her purse and brought out an envelope which she thrust into Angela's hands before any protest could be registered.

"I know you don't want any reward for your work with Jake, Angela, but I feel guilty because you have lost income with the time you devoted to him. Please accept this small token of our sincere appreciation. I truly don't know what I would have done without your help, my dear."

Angela could have refused, in light of the discoveries she had written about, and which she felt sure would lead to further work in the future, but one look at Susan's sincere, almost pleading, expression and she realized she could not disappoint this kind lady.

"Thank you so much," she said.

She turned to Maria for an especially close hug and kiss. "Tomorrow will be your last day here. I will stay on with Susan and Jake to complete his treatment. Anna will accompany them back to Canada and I will return to Italy then. It was so wonderful to see you at the villa, again. Please bring Lucy and Paul and your other daughter with the grandchildren next time."

"Oh, I certainly will! It was a magical time for me too!"

Angela climbed up the stairs to her bedroom and left the friends in the kitchen discussing the wedding and whether it was appropriate after such a night to have a cup of tea or another dram of whisky to celebrate.

☙❦☙

Sunday morning passed in a haze for the inhabitants of the McCaig Estate farmhouse.

Anna vaguely remembered the sound of Fiona's voice early, when it was scarcely light, but as soon as the front door closed again, she drifted back to a lovely dream of Bev and

Alan turning slowly to the strains of romantic music in the hotel ballroom.

Susan had risen early to add coal to the fire which Anna had banked down the night before. Susan had been given the instructions on appropriate feeding of the only heat source for the large room so she had trained herself to wake and check the fire's temperature from time to time during the night.

Immediately after she could see the flames were in evidence again, she scurried back to the warmth of the down-filled duvet and cuddled into Jake's back. He mumbled something indistinct and reached back to pat her leg before falling into a deep sleep.

For a moment, Susan lay, peacefully, listening to the crackle of coal. She felt drowsy but it had been such a wonderful night that she was reluctant to let the memories fade too fast.

There were no sounds from the rest of the house. Everyone would be sleeping late.

Her thoughts drifted to the lovely scenery around the farmhouse. They had not had much opportunity to explore this place where Anna had chosen to spend much of her time. Susan remembered Anna speaking about Helen's Hill behind the house and the extraordinary views of the surrounding country from the summit. Perhaps she could venture up there today?

There were choices to be made. It was their last day before departing for Toronto. Would it be possible to ask Fiona to take them on a drive around the area, possibly ending up in Oban? Fiona would be the perfect person to show them the scenery and point out the wildlife she had studied.

Yes! That was the answer! Susan determined to phone Fiona and set up this journey as soon as she could, without disturbing either Jake or Anna.

With this decision made, she slipped out of bed and quietly enveloped herself in a dressing gown Anna had supplied. She felt the cold air as she passed the front porch and quickly ran through and opened the door to the kitchen. A wave of warmth greeted her. The Aga cooker/come heating system, belted out its constant comfort as was proved by the amount of time Morag spent curled up on the rug in front of it. Susan stood on tiptoe to see if the cat was in her usual position and found Lucy there with Morag on her knees.

"Oh, Lucy! I forgot Fiona was going to bring you here early. Are you all right?"

"I'm fine, Aunt Susan, other than a bit stiff from all the dancing last night. Am I wrong or were those Scotsmen wearing black shorts under their kilts? I thought they went commando."

"I think that's one of those urban legends, Lucy," laughed Susan. "Would you like breakfast?"

"I've already eaten breakfast," came the reply. "There's no lazing around at Fiona's cottage, I can tell you. It's up with the larks for that lady, believe me!"

Lucy said this with such fervor that Susan suspected there had been a strict routine to be followed while Lucy stayed with Fiona.

She switched on the kettle and decided to prepare trays for the others when she noticed that Angela or Anna must have had the same impulse. Two trays were set with linen cloths and matching blue delft plates, cups and saucers. How nice to be taken care of by good friends, she thought, not for the first time.

She could see where Maria got her ambition and helpful nature. Angela, although a younger cousin, was clearly a member of the same family.

When tea was made, Lucy accepted a cup and soon shared a plate of toast with Susan. As they munched and spread butter and thick marmalade liberally, their conversation turned to the topic of their shared time in Italy. It was a new bond between them and Susan could see the change in Lucy's attitude to everything that had happened there, including matters between her and her mother.

"I've been thinking about something, Aunt Susan, and I want to ask your advice."

"Ask away, Lucy." Susan sipped tea and tried to hide her curiosity. There was no way to guess what topic Lucy was about to introduce and she hoped she could respond appropriately.

"Do you remember what happened when we were leaving the villa and the three old aunties of my Mom's gathered at the door?"

"Yes, they were all very sad to see us go. You especially, *Bella Lucia*!"

"Well, as it happens, that is exactly what I am wondering about. They gave me the medal of Saint Lucy. I've been wearing it ever since." Lucy drew the silver medallion out from under her sweater and it gleamed in the light from the huge glass windows.

"It's really beautiful, Lucy! Something very special from Verona for you to treasure."

"I know." Lucy pursed her lips as she considered what to say next. "I was thinking I would like to give the medal to Aunt Alina."

Susan gasped when she heard this. She had not expected the next sentence to go in this direction at all.

"Lucy, that's a generous thought! It's a very personal gift. Would you want to part with it?" Susan did not know if Lucy had been told about Alina's eye condition and she was reluctant to divulge the information in case the girl was not meant to know about it.

"I heard Mom talking about Aunt Alina and I felt so sad. The wedding dress was made by her, wasn't it? It was so delicate and perfect. I could cry to think she might not be able to do such amazing work in the future and I thought the medal would help in some small way just to tell her we all think about her."

Lucy stopped and looked at Susan to try to gauge her

reaction. She unconsciously twisted the chain of the medal as she waited for the result.

"I see what you are thinking, Lucy. The medal is meant to protect a person's sight. Am I correct?"

Lucy nodded and waited again.

"I am sure Alina would be most touched to have your medal, Lucy, and even more touched that you would think of her so highly. Ask your mother, to be sure it's OK with her, and thank you, my dear, for confiding in me."

"No problem, Aunt Susan. I've learned a lot about friendships on this holiday and I hope that one day I can have friends as close as you and Mom and Anna are."

"What's that about me, you two?" Anna descended the stairs into the kitchen, dressed for outdoors. "Ah, there's tea and toast! I could smell it from upstairs. I am going to sit here and eat while you get ready to go out, Susan. Jake and Angela have a scheduled session here today. I have called Fiona and she is at our disposal for anything you want to do or see. You can let me know your preference when you are ready to go. Meanwhile I will be grilling Lucy, here, about all the things she has been saying about me."

Lucy looked up in alarm to see if Anna was annoyed with her but the grin on her face belied the serious words. "It's time we had a little chat, Lucy. We have some catching up to do."

<hr/>

The tour of the area turned out to be a huge success. Fiona knew every back road to all the quaint villages and spectacular viewpoints. They drove down valleys, crossed bridges and followed rivers, then climbed up through mountain passes where the heather was still in bloom. The clear, crisp weather persisted and they could see for miles.

They saw a stag silhouetted against the sky on a craggy cliff and everyone stopped breathing for a minute, the sight was so magnificent. Lucy recovered first and in a swift move that her father would have approved, she took several photographs of the stag before he turned and vanished.

"That looked just like one of those old oil paintings in the hotel lobby!" she exclaimed, and the spell was broken. Everyone begged for copies of the photos and Lucy privately thought she might try a painting of her own, based on the images she had caught with the camera.

Later, Susan, sitting beside the driver, was the one who spotted an even more rare sight.

Soaring high above them was a huge bird with a vast wingspan. Fiona stopped the van and checked in the direction Susan indicated. She grabbed her binoculars and confirmed it was a sea eagle. Lucy was at the wrong side of the van but she quickly passed her camera forward to Fiona who swiftly zoomed in to capture the osprey in the lens.

Susan and Lucy exclaimed their delight that Fiona had arranged all these encounters with native life for them specially, but Anna knew that luck had played a large part in their good fortune. Nonetheless, she was pleased that her friends could now understand the appeal this beautiful land had for her. She was more certain every time she came to Oban that Helen had chosen well when she decided to settle in this area.

The tour ended at George and Jeanette's house where Maria was waiting to hear all about their adventures. She had spent the day with Jeanette and Liam, talking and laughing and enjoying the little boy's antics. Jeanette had a unique perspective on the local people which she shared with Maria when George was busy catching up with paperwork for a client.

"They can be mighty stubborn at times," she confessed, "but their hearts are as big as the ocean out there. They will help out anyone at all and they know when you sincerely like their country and the people in it. I often say it's a radar sense they have for phonies and cheats."

"But you like it here, Jeanette, don't you? You seem to have settled down very well."

"Oh, of course! It's not Canada but it does have its own charms, and now this wee lad is here, I can't imagine anywhere else I would rather be."

Maria could not help thinking about Theresa and her two little ones. Children made all the difference in life. A lot of work, but a blessing beyond compare.

A table was set in the dining room with a Scottish high tea for everyone. Salad and cold meats with potatoes smothered in parsley butter were accompanied by fresh-baked scones and a selection of cakes, pies and biscuits. Tea and coffee flowed freely from large pots and there was still plenty left when Catriona joined them on a break from the hotel to update them on the newly-married couple.

"They had breakfast in bed in their room this morn," she proclaimed, "and they went away to Skye for a few days honeymoon and to see Kirsty well settled. I was asked to extend their grateful thanks to all of you for making it an unforgettable night."

"I'll never forget it, that's for sure!" added Lucy. I think I want one of those energetic, high-stepping Scotsmen for myself, one of these days. "

Everyone in the room laughed in surprise but Maria wondered if her headstrong daughter really meant what she said. Now that they had established a closer relationship, the last thing she wanted was to lose her daughter to the general move eastward to Europe that Anna had started.

Chapter Twenty

✿❀✿

Maria and Lucy, faced a long, boring day of travel back to Canada.

They had bid fond farewells to Anna, Angela, Susan and Jake at a very early hour when Fiona arrived to take them to the train in Oban, on the first stage of their journey.

Susan and Jake would be joining them in a few days when Bev and Alan returned from their honeymoon to settle in their cottage home. Angela would depart for Italy on the same day, after completing Jake's treatment.

Anna wanted to stay in the farmhouse to keep an eye on Eric and James as they were alone in the cottage for the time being. She was determined to make sure the stockman, who was standing in for Alan, looked after the cows and sheep according to the standards of care set by their owners.

Prince, the sheepdog, was happy to stay with Eric or Anna but not sure yet of James when Eric was at school. Anna would happily walk Prince when Eric was not available.

She planned to feed the boys at her house and make certain both men and animals were well catered for. She also wanted to ensure that Susan and Jake were in the best possible shape for the journey home. It was good that she would be with them to lend a hand on the trip.

Philip could stay in Oban for only a day or two more. He and James would reverse their journey and drive back to Manchester where James would continue on to London by plane and Philip would fly back to join the team supervising his project in Egypt.

Anna had been delighted and surprised to see Philip arrive for the wedding but she regretted that their time together always seemed to be very brief. She determined to spend a few hours with Philip while she could, and discuss with him a much longer period when they could really get to know each other better. She had no intention of losing touch with this latest member of her family but where and when the reunion would take place was an unknown at the moment.

Plane travel west across the Atlantic had meant a long day flying in daylight. Few people slept, and the large airplane was full of chatter and movement. After a few hours Lucy grew tired of her iPod. The movies and TV programs were on such tiny screens, so far away from her, that she soon gave up on them also.

As they got closer to Canada, Lucy's thoughts moved to the future. It was an exciting prospect.

Her experiences in Italy had shown her new ways to blend her ideas with European style and flare. Now she had to put that knowledge into practice.

She turned to her mother with a concern she had wanted to discuss. "Mom, I really think you need to change the name of your store."

Maria had been lost in planning displays of the new clothes she had bought for the store and could not believe Lucy had tapped into her thoughts after several hours when they had not really spoken to each other.

"What's wrong with 'Maria's Modes'?" she asked. "It says who and what to expect inside. It is a very expensive thing to change letterhead and signage for a store when you have established a name, you know."

"I'm sure it *is* expensive, but, Mom, it's a really old-fashioned name and makes you sound as if you are a hundred years old, not the hip lady of today with far-out style."

Maria was both annoyed and pleased with this summary so she asked Lucy what store names she could suggest as a replacement, thinking this would stump her daughter and bring a close to the discussion.

"Well, I've been thinking about this, Mom. You know that motto you had painted on the back wall?"

"You mean; Fashion fades: Style remains?"

"Yes, that's the one! I think the store name should be something about style."

She paused and then continued while Maria waited to see what her daughter would come up with. "Something that references Style would fit better much better. What about Style Salon or Maria's Style Studio?"

"Hmm, sounds a bit like a hairstylist, Lucy. People might march in and insist on getting a haircut instead of buying new clothes."

"Well, choose something yourself, Mom, but Maria's Modes has to go, believe me."

Maria looked at her daughter. This concern with the store name was a new development.

What was behind her unexpected interest?

"Why do you care about this all of a sudden?" she challenged Lucy.

"Actually, I do have a good reason. I want to use a tiny corner of your store to start up a business of my own soon." Lucy saw her mother's jaw drop at this news and continued in a rush before she could refuse to discuss it any further. "I just want to set up a mannequin directed at teens who want to be fashionable without paying the kind of prices their mothers pay. When your clients come to the store they could bring their daughters and they would have something neat to look at while the parent is busy with you. You never know, it could help your sales and I could get a toe in the door, so to speak." Lucy ran out of breath at this point and waited apprehensively for her mother's reaction.

Maria's first instinct was to say no, emphatically, but she stopped herself just in time and remembered that this was a new beginning with Lucy and shooting down her ideas was not going to work any longer.

"What sort of space would you need and what would the mannequin be wearing?"

Lucy was astonished at this response and lost no time in capitalizing on what could only be a moment of weakness on her mother's part.

"I could do most of the preparation from home so I don't need much space in a stockroom. The clothes would be sharp-looking and up-to-date but with a vintage, recycling, repurposing approach, similar to what I do with my own clothes."

"Would you have the time to keep current with this once you are back at school and involved with your busy social calendar, Lucy? I don't want to encourage you now and find out in two months that you have lost interest altogether."

Lucy's heart was pounding at the thought her mother was close to accepting this idea. She began to promise the world but her practical mother intervened.

"*If* this is going to work, we need to put it on a business level with conditions on each side, a time frame, and a review after a specific period so either of us can withdraw if things don't work out."

"Oh, anything you want, Mom! You can trust my ideas now that I've seen what European fashion is really like. I won't let you down."

"What I *want* is a business plan answering some basic questions about what you intend to do, when you will do it and what your plans are if this idea takes off and you are faced with orders you can't fill."

This practical approach brought Lucy's flight of fancy to a crashing halt, but only for a moment. She had learned to appreciate her mother's business thinking in a way she never had before, but she wanted this opportunity badly and she would agree to anything that made it possible.

"I'm not finished, Lucy!" cautioned her mother. "You will, of course, have to keep up with your school work and help around the house more than you have done lately, and I don't want you to neglect other things in your life like your interest in painting for example."

"Don't worry! I have already discussed that with Aunt Anna and she says I can do it all if I get organized. She says the A Plus seamstresses might be able to do some work for me if I get requests for clothes."

"Aha! So that's where this is coming from! Anna has been encouraging you."

Lucy was unsure how her mother was reacting to Anna's role in this project so she jumped in again to smooth the waters. "Really, it's fine! Aunt Anna asked me about school and that led to a talk about the future and I do want to get going on this, Mom. I'm not getting any younger and some famous fashion designers started well before my age, you know."

Lucy's fervent plea made Maria want to laugh out loud. Privately she thought Lucy was more likely to be snapped up as a runway model than succeed in the very competitive game of fashion design. There was, however, the passion in Lucy's voice to consider and Maria could now see past the disadvantages of having a teenager and her friends inter-fering in her domain, to the chance to spend more time with her younger daughter and help her along the way to indepen-dence in whatever field she finally chose.

"Very well, I'll consider it," she responded, after a few

more moments. "But you have to get started on your business plan right away, young lady!"

"Yes, Ma'am!" said Lucy with a mock salute. "And will you also consider a new name for the store?"

Maria smiled a Mona Lisa smile and leaned back in her seat. "I will do that if you get some details down on paper before this plane lands in Toronto."

At least, she said to herself, I'll have peace and quiet for the next hour or so. And with this, Maria closed her eyes and slept. Her last conscious thought was, "Soon we will be home."

❦

Paul marched restlessly up and down the Arrivals hall at Pearson Airport.

Theresa watched him and thought he had not adjusted yet to the time difference in south-western Ontario. He had been fidgeting the whole way here in the car and had hustled her out of the downtown hotel almost as soon as they had found their rooms and put down their luggage.

Personally, she was relishing this break from home and kids; especially now that she was out of a job. She felt guilty every day when Joe trudged off to work. She knew he was worried about money and nothing she had tried so far had given her any reason to hope there would be work for her on the horizon. London's college and university students had already nabbed all the part-time Christmas seasonal jobs.

There was always plenty to do at home, of course, but that kind of work was repetitive and endless. When she had worked part-time, those few hours away had brought a new perspective to her daily tasks and the thought of being paid at the end of two weeks was a great incentive. It meant she could buy the odd little luxury for the kids without having to explain the expense to Joe when the bills came in.

Theresa shuffled around in her hard plastic seat. She could

see the lines of weary travellers emerging from the exit and pushing carts full of their luggage along the barriers to the open area where family and friends waited eagerly to enfold them in welcoming arms.

Theresa was not sure how welcoming she felt towards her mother and Lucy. Because she had missed her mother's comforting reassurances about being fired, a tiny part of her still blamed Lucy for taking their mother away just when she was most needed. She could already feel the resentment building toward Lucy. I had better watch my tongue, she warned herself. With both Mom and Pops here, I need to be on my best behaviour. I promised to put the jealousy aside for everyone's benefit, and that includes mine, too. I know it, but making it work is hard.

Her father seemed to have run out of patience. As Theresa watched, he slipped around the barrier and peered through the crowd to find the rest of his family. Maria was easy to spot with her dark, shiny cap of hair and the elegant posture that no amount of travel fatigue could diminish. He sighed with relief and grabbed her as soon as she reached him, wrapping his arms around her slim frame until he had her in a bear hug so he could whisper in her ear, "My Maria, my darling! How I have missed you!"

Lucy slid past and pulled forward her wheeled case with the package of paintings strapped to the extended handles. Her turn with her father would come later.

Theresa spotted her sister in the crowd and had to look again to be sure. What had happened to Lucy? She looked different, somehow. Theresa began to examine her sister in detail, attempting to zero in on what made the difference.

Same long dark hair swinging around her face. Very sharp new leather jacket over her jeans, but that wasn't it. New boots? No, not that either.

Lucy waved and smiled at Theresa. Wow! She smiled at me. That's different! Then Theresa put all the parts together and made a whole. Lucy's fingernails were pale instead of the black polish she had favoured for months. Her entire face seemed brighter and lighter and Theresa did not believe a new, less-mask-like make-up could be the only cause. She just looked more relaxed, more mature, more *present* in some strange way. It seemed like her nuisance of a little sister had changed.

Maybe this new Lucy would be less selfish and more willing to be an active part of the family.

Theresa could certainly do with the support from a sister in the coming months. She decided to put aside her resentment and start this new phase off in the right way by smiling back and walking over to meet Lucy. Before she could say a word, however, Lucy started to talk at her usual rapid rate but with an enthusiastic voice that also sounded new to Theresa.

"Hi there, sis! It's great to see you! I've so much to tell you, Theresa! I have learned so much about everything and everyone, not least of all myself. You won't believe the stuff I have done, and now I see you I realize how much I have missed you and the kids. Come over her and give me a hug!"

Maria eventually untangled herself from Paul's embrace and relinquished her case to his strong arms. She hefted her carry-on bag but kept one arm free to grasp him around his waist. The two were one again and she had someone to share decisions and triumphs with.

"Well, was the trip worth it?" he asked. Maria looked up into his bright eyes and felt at home.

"Yes!" she answered, "worthwhile in so many ways, Paul. I have plans to tell you about. There will be changes from now on. My aim is to bring balance back to all of us."

"That sounds extremely hopeful, my darling. You can tell me all about it at the hotel I have booked for us. I have news for you, too; a serious job offer for a change. We should be secure for the next year, at least."

Perfect, thought Maria as she tightened her grip on Paul. A year will be enough time for us to become the family we should have been from the start. I will definitely spend more time with Theresa and the children and make sure she knows how much I value her. How lovely that Paul brought her here to meet us. And Paul has booked a hotel for us to rest up in. We'll have time to spend with my parents and enjoy their surprise when Lucy presents the paintings. So many good things for us to look forward to. Oh, it's so good to be home again!

She looked ahead and saw Theresa and Lucy with their heads together, chatting and laughing like the sisters and friends they should always be.

There were decisions to be made to create the future Maria wanted, but, for once she felt equipped and confident to make these decisions for herself and her whole family. It was as if she had been granted a reprieve; a step back from the edge that meant there was renewed hope for a better life.

She thought about how she and Lucy, Susan and Jake had travelled to Italy for very different reasons. Each one was returning home changed in some significant way. It seemed that friendship was the strong link that tied their fates together.

Life was good; family and friends were essential; work was satisfying; the future looked bright and Maria walked forward, together with her husband, to welcome it.

THE END.

The Prime Time Series continues in *Sand in the Wind*, book 4.

Afterword

Prime Time was my first series. I was hoping to find readers in the *prime* of their lives with *time* to read captivating stories, set in real-life locations and featuring women you would like to get to know.

Anna Mason is that woman. She is at a crossroads in her life when she gets a chance to take a new direction and travel to Scotland with the encouragement of her group of faithful friends.

This series is now eight full books and Anna is still going strong with adventures that will transport you to places you might never expect. You will fall in love with Anna, as I have.

Read Ruth's other series, Seafarers, Seven Days, Home Sweet Home, Journey of a Lifetime and Starscopes at retailers everywhere. Also read Borderlines a stand-alone thriller.

www.ruthhay.com

Also by Ruth Hay

Prime Time Series

Auld Acquaintance

Time Out of Mind

Now or Never

Sand in the Wind

With This Ring

The Seas Between Us

Return to Oban: Anna's Next Chapter

Fiona of Glenmorie

Seafarers Series

Sea Changes

Sea Tides

Gwen's Gentleman

Gwen's Choice

Seven Days Series

Seven Days There

Seven Days Back

Seven Days Beyond

Seven Days Away

Seven Days Horizons

Seven Days Destinations

Borderlines (Standalone)

Borderlines

Home Sweet Home Series

Harmony House

Fantasy House

Remedy House

Affinity House

Memory House

Journey of a Lifetime Series

Auralie

Nadine

Mariette

Rosalind

Starscopes Series

Starscopes: Winter

Starscopes: Spring

Starscopes: Summer

Starscopes: Fall

Made in the USA
Monee, IL
08 May 2020

29974238R00111